MUDDY SPIRITS

JESSICA TASTET

Publications

MUDDY SPIRITS

A Raleigh Cheramie Mystery

By
Jessica Tastet

Dandelion Wish Publications

Muddy Spirits

Copyright May 2022 Jessica Tastet

Cover Design by Ashley Comeaux-Foret

ISBN 978-1-7362439-3-0

ISBN 978-1-7362439-4-7

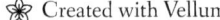 Created with Vellum

CHAPTER ONE

"Have you had an opportunity to study the foyer mural?" Horace Dantin droned on, his tone as nasal and snooty as his awareness that no one wanted to listen to his endless drivel.

While waiting for Sheri to return, Raleigh Cheramie had been unfortunate to be cornered by the pretentious soon-to-be relative of her friend. He'd tried every guest at the engagement party in hopes of sharing stories of the manor's history. Even though time and time again, they'd excused themselves from the conversation, he still didn't understand that no one wanted to hear it.

While he rambled on about vibrant colors and traditional painting techniques, Raleigh scanned the ballroom, searching for an escape from this painful conversation.

Boyfriend Mike Simmons did not appear among the faces of the guests as all the groomsmen had escaped a half hour ago and had not returned. Nate had mentioned something about a boxing match. Luckily, Sheri had missed the conversation while Horace was informing her about the updates fifty years ago to the ballroom. Sheri hadn't turned into a bridezilla by any means, but a MIA groom could be problematic.

Not seeing any of the other bridesmaids, Raleigh considered enlisting her sister's help. Currently, Madison worked behind the bar area. Three hours into the party, a line had formed for the beer and wine. From the decibel level and the dancing of this crowd, Madison should probably tell them the alcohol had dried out. Her sister seemed agitated and more likely to toss a drink at a guest than tell them no, which is why she didn't typically serve the drinks. Continuing her scan, Raleigh found the new hire for Madison's party business standing in stilettos near a topiary flirting with Sheri's cousin Jerry. As Raleigh watched, the young woman ran a finger down Jerry's chest and leaned in close to his ear. Raleigh guessed they'd be ducking off soon. Raleigh should probably go and help Madison, maybe commiserate with her on the unreliability of employees. But Raleigh and Madison didn't really have that kind of relationship, and Madison preferred keeping a distance so if she ended up dancing on top of a bar, Raleigh didn't drag her scantily clad butt off. It's how their sisterhood worked without the two murdering each other. Besides, as the maid of honor, Raleigh should at least be able to enjoy all the parties and hoopla. She'd have to escape the manor's historian first.

"That mural is original to the house," Horace continued, his large forehead wrinkled in emphasis. "Painted by our very own patriarch, my grandfather."

Raleigh nodded, keeping her opinion to herself. She believed the whole scene of shooting and skinning an alligator grotesque as a first impression when walking into a home of this magnitude. But what did she know? The only art she could afford was her six-year-old nephew's sketches of trees that looked like fuzzy squirrel tails.

The groom Jeff Dantin's grandmother, Eliza Dantin, belonged to one of the old money families of Barbeaux Bayou.

In the early 1900s, the family had bought into the shipping industry. They'd sold out only a few years ago, but the sale had made them even wealthier. The family's southern manor stood as a testament to the time when the family had reached its summit. Equipped with its own ballroom and six bedrooms, the gawdy monstrosity of a house stood too large for the two people remaining residents. Neither the family's matriarch nor Horace seemed ready to abandon the family home though.

"Perhaps when the place belongs to me," Horace rambled completely unaware of his audience's disinterest. "I can open it up for events such as this. Then everyone will see our family's good taste."

Raleigh's eyebrow arched and she turned away quickly so he wouldn't see her disapproval. During the entire wedding planning process, Sheri had attempted to play nice with the future-in-laws. Sheri's own family tended to be a train wreck, so the effort had gone into smoothing the edges between the two families. Raleigh didn't want to cause a derailment, especially during the holiday season when everyone aimed for grace, but tensions ran high.

With only two days before Christmas, Raleigh could extend Christmas spirit to even Horace's over inflated ego.

"I see you are counting me out already." A sharp, shrill voice spoke from behind her, causing Raleigh to turn.

A petite woman in a navy-blue beaded ball gown hobbled her last two steps toward them, her carved cane leading the way. Even as the woman neared a century, her upswept gray hair held hints of the black it had once been. Impeccably dressed, her drawn in eyebrows were raised at her son.

"No, mother," Horace stuttered, looking down at his black loafers.

Grand'Mere Eliza Lydia Dantin shook her head and

focused on Raleigh. "He always forgets that he only inherits if a girl isn't born into the family."

Horace tssked. "Much too late for that to happen now. We aren't having any children at our age."

Eliza Dantin smiled in amusement, leaning on the curve of her cane. "My son always counts the ladies out. Aren't we marrying one of my grandsons in three days?"

Horace drew back, appalled. "We're counting great grand-children now. Surely Sheri would not want another child with hers being so old. She's not getting any younger either."

Cringing, Raleigh bit down on her bottom lip. Shawn may have turned ten at his last birthday party, but she and Sheri happened to be the same age. She'd been called old at 30. Paw would say Horace had skipped the commonsense line at birth, but the man's insult didn't sting any less.

"Nonsense," Eliza said, pulling her tiny body up straight. "Not to mention insulting. Where is the bride to be? Perhaps we should ask her about her plans instead of gossiping."

Raleigh scanned the room again and didn't see her. In fact, the bride had disappeared a while ago. "How about I go and find her?"

Eliza smiled and nodded as if that had been her point all along. Raleigh left the two, hearing Horace's nasally voice following her as he pleaded with his mother to take it easy tonight. The ballroom had been stuffed with poinsettia and spruce tree arrangements that indicated a Christmas soiree more than engagement party. The soft 3-piece jazz band on the center stage did not drown out the deep voice of Sheri's uncle as he said, "They have more money than they know what to do with. They won't miss a statue."

Raleigh walked by without eyeing said statue, not wanting to be a witness in what would certainly be a family scandal.

Sheri's Uncle Cedric had served five years in his younger days for robbing a convenience store. He claimed he'd been in uncontrollable circumstances. Sheri said those circumstances involved a case of beer a day chased down by a joint or two a day habit. Old habits died hard, especially in Barbeaux Bayou where they typically went to curl up and collect dust.

Raleigh headed in the direction of the kitchens, thinking Sheri had said she was going to refill her glass from the coolers. The bride had made a special concoction that she'd read would not cause puffiness or hangovers. Raleigh didn't want to burst her bridal bubble that the only drink that could possibly deliver on that promise was water. All brides should be able to believe in wedding cake with no calories and receptions with no family drama.

In the kitchens she only found the two other bridesmaids proposing a sloppy toast to each other having the marriage portion of their life to-do lists out of the way already.

"I think Sheri went to the bathroom," Elizabeth said, pausing in her sip to consider the question. As the groom's stepsister, Elizabeth had been the obligatory pick for bridesmaid. Although Sheri did seem to genuinely like her future sister-in-law.

"No," Stephanie corrected. "Her dress. She had to go fix the strap on her dress."

Stephanie had enjoyed best friend status in high school. She and Sheri rarely spent more time than her monthly salon appointment now. But when the woman had found out about Sheri and Jeff's engagement, she'd declared herself a bridesmaid because of a promise made back in eighth grade at a slumber party. Sheri had said that it was too strange to even argue with the woman.

Turning down an offer for a glass of champagne, Raleigh

headed toward the upstairs bedrooms. For the wedding week, Sheri had been staying at the manor to help with the wedding details but also to honor Jeff's family wishes of them not living together before the wedding. Since Sheri's mom and dad had been divorced since she was two years old, Raleigh could imagine that Jeff's family had issues on many levels that they struggled with besides the fact that the two had been living together for three months.

The first bedroom door stood open and two young girls sat at a vanity playing with jewelry. Their brunette and blonde heads leaned in so close they touched as they ran tiny fingers over opalescent pearls.

Raleigh caught a glimpse of herself in the low mirror and could see that the curls that Madison had set in her normally stick straight brunette hair had begun to lose their bounce. They did at least wave, so that was a plus. Raleigh had no words for the dark eye shadow and make up her sister had layered on her otherwise fair complexion, but it did make her green eyes "pop" like her sister had assured her.

Raleigh slid away from her reflection not wanting to look at that mess anymore. She realized much too late that Madison had made her look like her. Not the look Raleigh would ever willingly aim for.

"Have you two seen the bride by chance?" Raleigh asked.

Startled, they grabbed for the string of pearls as they turned toward Raleigh.

"I tell you what," Raleigh said, winking at them. "I won't tell anyone what I saw if you tell me where I can find Sheri."

The pale blonde with the deep blue eyes stared at her before saying, "She's in the room across the hall crying."

Raleigh smiled, backing out of the room. "Just be gentle, girls. A string of pearls can break easily. But they are beautiful."

They dissolved into a fit of giggles as Raleigh left, closing the door behind her.

Raleigh knocked on the mirror image door across the hall and heard a muffled, "I'm indisposed."

Recognizing Sheri's voice, although distant, she opened the door anyway.

Unlike the twin canopy beds across the hall, the ivory striped walls of this room held an antique four poster bed covered with plush satin bedding. Empty of Sheri though. Raleigh walked toward the ajar bathroom door leading to an ensuite.

Pushing the door open, Raleigh discovered Sheri crumpled on a plush white rug. The silver touches and modern tile gave away the attempt to modernize a house built at a time when closets and inside bathrooms didn't exist. The space would not allow for more than one person to fit, however.

With tear smudges, Sheri looked up, her eyes panic stricken. "I can't do this."

A chord of panic strummed through Raleigh. "Can't do what exactly?"

Sheri's tears spilled over. "I can't get married. I just can't."

Pulling the hem of the red satin dress up, Raleigh sank down onto the plush carpet. She'd borrowed this overpriced, much too fancy number from Madison, and her sister would be murderous if she permanently damaged the dress, even if it were for a good cause.

"What's going on? Did Jeff do something? Say something?"

"No," Sheri cried harder. "I'm pregnant."

Raleigh didn't follow her train of thought yet, but she'd heard pregnancy hormones could make a woman crazy. Maybe that's what was happening here. "And Jeff doesn't want a baby?"

"He's thrilled," Sheri gasped for air. "We moved up the

wedding because he had this idea to tell everyone for New Year's."

"Honey," Raleigh said, reaching over and patting her bare leg. "I'm not understanding the problem yet. Jeff's a great guy. Honestly, I thought he'd be a confirmed bachelor, but he's happy. He loves your son, too."

"This morning's ultrasound showed we are having a girl," Sheri wailed.

Raleigh scrutinized Sheri's loose fitting ivory dress with its fur shawl and lace sleeves. Although Sheri had always been on the plus size, she didn't look far enough along in a pregnancy to be having a gender ultrasound.

"Exactly how pregnant are we talking?" Raleigh asked.

"Sixteen weeks and two days," Sheri gushed. "It's been so hard to keep it secret, but Jeff wanted to be married first. His family are staunchly catholic. Church every Sunday. You know the type? I couldn't get him to understand that it won't matter because I couldn't change the due date. I gave in because it made him happy." She shrugged, dabbing at her eyes with a piece of toilet paper.

Raleigh heard a shuffle in the hall. When she looked back no one had entered the bedroom, so she figured the two girls had grown bored of the jewelry and rejoined the party.

"And he doesn't want a girl?" Raleigh asked still attempting to identify the problem.

Sheri shook her head. She leaned in and spoke in a lowered voice. "All the girls in Jeff's family die."

Raleigh exhaled, biting her tongue against saying aloud "nonsense." Instead, she asked,

"What do you mean?"

Sheri reached behind her, grabbing more toilet paper to begin vigorously wiping at the black streaks running down her cheeks. "There are no girls in the family because they have all tragically died. Grand'Mere Eliza's daughter died in an accident at seven years old and then Jeff's sister drowned. Supposedly Horace's wife gave birth to a stillborn girl."

Raleigh released an uneasy breath. Hormones. It had to be. As resident traiteur to the dead, she'd declared a vacation for Christmas holidays. No mystical funny stuff. As a member of the family of Cajun folk healers for their community, most residents didn't agree as Me'Maw fondly reminded her. "Just because those awful things happened doesn't mean anything will happen to your little girl."

"How do I know though?" Sheri's eyes widened. "How do I take the chance? The family claims it's a curse."

Raleigh's thoughts grasped at the idea. She'd heard many unbelievable stories in her time. "Your baby belongs to this family regardless of if you marry Jeff or not..."

"Oh my God!" Sheri exclaimed, clutching the tissue to her mouth.

"So, I suggest," Raleigh continued, "I look into it and see if it's actually a family curse or just bad luck."

"But the wedding is in three days!" Sheri exclaimed.

Raleigh focused on her friend. "Do you love Jeff?"

Sheri nodded, her bottom lip trembling.

"Then there isn't an issue," Raleigh said. "He will want to protect your baby as much as you."

"There you two are," Madison exclaimed from the door-frame of the bedroom entrance. "It's time for bridal party toasts. It is taking forever to collect everyone."

Frazzled, Madison was completely unaware that she'd interrupted a conversation. The stress of a growing business had caused some regression on the social etiquette Raleigh had thought her sister was developing.

Sheri groaned.

Raleigh extended her hand and stood up. "Let's fix your eye make-up and toast to your future happiness."

Sheri hesitated, but then accepted her hand.

Raleigh could deal with family curses all day long as long as the dying didn't pay her a visit and insist she offer assistance. She'd hoped for a normal Christmas and a smooth wedding.

She was determined to have both.

CHAPTER TWO

By the time Raleigh sank into a deep sleep on her feather mattress, her calves and feet ached, and the three chocolate martinis had run through her body only adding to her exhaustion. Her body's decent into slumber caused the tapping to permeate through her dream first, causing her heart to race. The fear lured her from the darkness and made her realize that the sound came insistently from downstairs.

Groaning, she pulled her pillow over her face, inhaling goose down and the lingering scent of lavender pillow spray. The sound only increased.

No one would be visiting in the middle of the night. No one respectable. Which is why it must be her Great Aunt Clarice. The resident ghost of the house.

Perhaps she needed to investigate ways to exorcise a ghost from a home.

As she trudged downstairs, she considered all the words she could use to express her displeasure with Aunt Clarice. None of these would make Me'Maw happy with her manners, even if it were three in the morning and completely understandable.

The mischievous woman stood in the front doorway, a slight smile on her stained lips.

"Took you long enough."

Raleigh glared at her. As usual, the woman chose to appear in her late twenties, not the version Raleigh had known in her own lifetime. Of course, twenty-nine-year-old Aunt Clarice wore a form fitting dress in loud colors, impeccably upswept hair, and a sequined red beret tonight as a finishing Christmas touch. The woman looked like she'd stepped out of an old Hollywood glamour pin-up shoot.

Raleigh made a move toward the living room and grumbled, "Nothing is good enough to have me up at this time."

"No sit down tete-a-tete tonight, darlin'," Aunt Clarice chimed. "We are going on a field trip."

Her words caused Raleigh to step back. Field trip? No one would be accepting visitors at this time in Barbeaux Bayou. Even the bars had closed an hour ago.

"You're kidding, right?" Raleigh asked.

Aunt Clarice's laugh fluttered. "No laughs tonight, kiddo. We have been given a mission, and we need to get to it."

"A what?" Raleigh asked. She inhaled deeply, trying to clear the fogginess of sleep from her brain. Those martinis made it difficult.

"Come on, darlin'," Aunt Clarice motioned her toward the front door. "The night isn't getting any younger and neither are you."

Raleigh grunted, but she still moved toward the door. The woman could be annoying, but she'd always been right. Raleigh blinked as blackness descended around her, and when her eyes opened sunlight blinded her from above. She and Aunt Clarice stood at the edge of the landscaped yard of the Dantin's Manor. Raleigh recognized the south terrace and the courtyard off the den. The area did lack the pool and pool cabana though that had been there only a few hours ago when she'd left the home.

Surveying the area, Raleigh saw a massive treehouse with a lone swing hanging from a branch of a century old oak tree. She didn't recall the structure or tree being among the string lights and gas firepits. Had she missed these? Not possible. The tree had been removed at some point. Which caused warning signs to begin to vibrate through Raleigh.

With a shrieking entrance, children ran through the yard chasing each other. Alarmed, Raleigh looked for cover to duck behind, unsure how this journey worked. Her usual traiteur to the dead connections involved her slipping into their bodies as they died, so she never had to worry about having witnesses. As a ghost, Aunt Clarice had no concerns about any of this.

"Don't worry dear," Aunt Clarice said, her form shimmering under the sun. "No one can see us. It's a mission perk."

"What is this mission?" Raleigh asked flustered. Missions didn't feel like something she should use her vacation days for, and ghostly duties certainly didn't feel like Christmas cheer and wedding celebrations.

Aunt Clarice shrugged. "We are here to help Sheri."

Pregnancy worries didn't seem worth middle of the night covert missions. Unless there was something more to the supposed Dantin curse.

As the children ran only feet in front of them, Raleigh recognized the brunette girl who'd played with the pearl necklace in the upstairs bedroom last night. Her curls tumbled around her shoulders and her face lit with merriment as the slightly overweight boy trailed behind her.

Neither of them offered she and Aunt Clarice any attention as they passed. The girl sped toward the treehouse, shrieking as she sprinted.

For the first time since the tapping began back in her own

bedroom, Raleigh's brain chugged into a normal speed. Warning flags began to rise that something wasn't right.

As the boy passed her, she took in his wide forehead and his spreading nostrils, and she gasped.

"What year is this?" Raleigh asked, a feeling of panic seized her that she hadn't felt since her early years of becoming traiteur to the dead when it had all been new and frightening.

Aunt Clarice chuckled. "Oh, I believe we went back fifty years or so to a time when this body was flesh and raging hormones."

Horace Dantin.

Raleigh watched as the girl nimbly climbed the rope ladder up the tree. She moved easily as if her fingers and toes were fly paper. She disappeared inside the rugged wood structure just as Horace reached the base of the tree. His fleshy arms struggled with the rope. His upper body strength had not caught up to his size. At ten or so, puberty had not caused his body to slim out into the medium built man she'd found annoying last night.

After a struggle to reach the top, he whined for Claudette to come and help him. To climb into the trap door required upper body strength—something his out of breath, red-faced self could not muster.

Raleigh held her breath, feeling as if he'd fall. His arms giving up on him.

Claudette laughed, the sound of garden chimes, but her tiny hand reached out from the inside.

He clutched at her hand—or did he pull?

Claudette dropped from the opening and landed in a heap on the ground. She released a little gasp before the thud echoed around them.

Raleigh bolted toward her, but Aunt Clarice put a cold hand on her arm to hold her in place.

Others came running. An old frumpy housekeeper who'd been hanging laundry behind an old wash shed screeched and began yelling for help. A gardener who had been trimming trees beyond the fence line hopped over the fence and skirted over to her.

Horace had slowly climbed down from the tree, keeping a safe distance back from the entire incident. Now, he trailed behind the ensemble into the house.

Sheri's words from the bathroom came back to Raleigh, and her pulse quickened. *Eliza's daughter had died.*

Raleigh looked down as Aunt Clarice touched her forearm with a cold palm. Her grip caused blackness to descend around them, but when Raleigh blinked against the rising panic, they were inside the front sitting room that they'd seen as they entered the grand foyer of the manor last night. The one with its archway facing the grand staircase to the ballroom. The navy-blue silk draperies were pulled closed, and the furniture appeared stiff, even though the cotton blue coloring attempted at warmth and welcome.

Eliza slumped in a wing back chair, a delicate lace handkerchief clutched in her hand. "I just know the boy did it on purpose. He was always jealous."

A tall stiff gentleman in a black suit sighed as he did a quarter turn away from a formal portrait of a large steamboat. "You must not say those things, Eliza. He's our son."

"She was my perfect child," Eliza wailed, rocking back and forth in her chair. "Only seven years old. How could he take her from me?"

The gentleman crossed to her, leaving the steamboat painting hanging above the old radio behind. He knelt in front of her and gathered her hands in his. "We have three other children. All fine sons who need you to keep it together."

"I want my daughter back!" Eliza wailed.

Her husband tightened his grip on her hands. "I want her back too, but we can't change circumstances."

"I want another girl," Eliza said, dabbing her face with the handkerchief, her voice rising in desperation.

"You know Doc Thibodaux said you shouldn't have any more babies after Claudette," her husband said, his tone gentle.

"Fine," Eliza exclaimed. "Then, I want only a future girl of our family to inherit the manor."

"Eliza," his tone cautioned.

"My father built this home," Eliza said, her tone stubborn. "And I inherited it because he said girls rarely get treated fairly in life. They are usually at the mercy of men just like my Claudette. A brother who failed her, a doctor who couldn't save her. A cruel world for girls. Our sons will be fine." Her tone turned bitter. "They all seem to be ruthless Dantin family members like their ancestors."

Husband sighed, releasing her hands. "And what happens if there are no girls?"

"We can donate it to the church." Eliza declared.

Husband shook his head. "I'll compromise. The first girl born can be named as inheritor, but if that doesn't happen, our eldest son can have it."

Eliza scoffed. "He wants to be a priest. He will donate it to the church anyway."

"True," husband said, "so how about the son who marries and continues the family name?"

Eliza didn't look at him. "I miss Claudette. I feel like she's here with me. I can smell her sometimes. The soap and the grass that she always smelled of. I want to hold her."

"I know, sweetheart," Alfredo soothed. "Her spirit was just too much for this world."

Hearing a scuffle behind her, Raleigh turned and caught two little boys peeking around the corner near the doorway.

One was Horace, and the other held a strong resemblance to Jeff, except for the brown eyes. The two brothers who stood an inch or so apart pushed at each other to get the better listening advantage.

At the bottom of the staircase stood the faint outline of Claudette watching them all.

In this form, there was no mistaken the girl for a spirit, unlike last night when Raleigh had thought she'd stumbled upon corporeal children. There was also no mistake that this girl did not share the same happiness and joy that the girl that had just ran past her outside in whatever memory Aunt Clarice had landed them in.

This girl looked angry. Vengeful even.

CHAPTER THREE

With a start, Raleigh sat up in bed, tugging at the sheet and comforter tangled around her legs and torso. She tried to remember how she'd returned to her nice comfortable bed, but she only recalled the girl by the staircase that last night at the party she'd mistaken for a living child. She didn't remember climbing back in bed or even when she'd returned.

Had she dreamed the entire experience? Perhaps Sheri's conversation had penetrated through her subconscious and created a horrible nightmare.

Raleigh looked at the bridesmaid's dress hanging from the frame of her closet. Even the reassurance that the dress wasn't hideous didn't distract her from the night's events. Her luck didn't run on the side of the episode being a figment of her imagination. She'd been warned that once she embraced her talents they would expand. This felt like an expansion.

Besides from mistaking a ghost child for a real kid, growth of her ability was the most disturbing take-away from the last twenty-four hours. Losing touch with reality felt like a possibility in the future if she couldn't tell the difference between a ghost and a person.

She'd only confirm people's suspicions that she'd gone crazy.

Raleigh glanced over at the alarm clock and the lateness of the hour sunk through her self-indulgent worries. Lunging out of bed, kicking her foot from the comforter, she hurried toward the shower, figuring she could stress over the night's events as she tried not to be late for the day's itinerary.

This week had been filled with pre-wedding festivities, and today was no different. At one o'clock Eliza would be hosting a lady's Christmas Cookie tea. As a maid of honor, Raleigh had been assigned the duty of picking up cookies from the downtown bakery, which closed at noon today on account of it being a holiday.

With eight minutes to spare, Raleigh parallel parked in front of *Sweet Tooth,* Helena Dardar's bakery.

Aiming an "overslept" in Reggie's direction, she hurried toward the sweet's case. Reggie continued cleaning the tiny bistro tables while watching Helena frown and regard Raleigh with disgust. She did go to the cases behind the counter though and begin retrieving trays of beautifully iced tea cookies in various Christmas shapes.

As she placed the last box on the counter, Helena commented, "I didn't think Sheri one for all this fanciness."

Raleigh watched Helena fiddle with the rack of individually boxed cupcakes. "The parties are hosted by the family. She planned a simple wedding. I mean no plain dresses for Sheri, but also no orchestra and five course meal for the reception either."

Helena nodded. "The girl got lucky snagging Jeff."

Raleigh frowned. "I think Jeff feels pretty lucky, too."

Helena turned away as she returned an empty tray to a cart behind the counter.

Barbeaux was nothing without its judgyness and its gossip, and Helena had held onto some bitterness after Madison's reality show had exposed her secret relationship. The girl may be bitter, but she made the best sweets in town.

With her hands on the filled boxes, Raleigh turned. "Reggie, help me load all of this up, so I can get out your way."

Dropping his rag, Reggie scuttled over, avoiding Helena's glare. Since Reggie had been in Raleigh's sister's kindergarten class and had trailed behind the collected rag tag group of rebels that Madison had collected like a puppy dog, Raleigh had known the man practically his entire life. Recently, Raleigh had heard about some trouble and a few months in rehab after a felony theft charge. The bakery job had to be part of some agreement or service hours or at least a way to earn his way back into the good grace of someone. A few years ago, he'd been in real estate, and Helena certainly couldn't be a nice boss. Madison should probably hire him. He'd likely be much more help than what she had now.

Grabbing two of the four trays, Reggie followed Raleigh to the back seat of her small sedan.

"How's Madison?" Reggie asked after closing the back passenger door.

"Business is booming," Raleigh said. "You should ask her for a job. She certainly could use reliable help."

Reggie's cheeks pinkened. "Might be awkward with that embarrassing crush I had on her growing up."

Raleigh closed her own door and stepped onto the sidewalk. "You two are nearly 25 now. I think it will be okay."

"I'll consider it." He grinned.

A short time later, Raleigh made it to the land of the elite, meaning the sprawling outskirts of Barbeaux where the homes sat on more than seventy-five feet long lots. Here, homes that could claim hers as a guest house sat on acres of land with sweeping oaks and bayou views—houses Raleigh's little Acadian cottage could only dream of growing up to be one day. She'd have to settle for one day paying off the mortgage of her own piece of Cheramie Lane.

At the Dantin Manor, a housekeeper wearing a frumpy gray dress greeted her at the door and helped her unload the trays. She only tssked once about Raleigh's late arrival.

The two carried them into the now cordoned ballroom. Oversized partitions on rollers slid across to cut last night's ballroom in half, offering the tea social a more intimate feel. Noisily rolling in silver tea trolleys, Madison wore an expression of a soldier entering battle.

Carrying cookie trays, Raleigh followed the housekeeper toward the overburdened serving tables. "Aren't you supposed to be a guest today?"

"Yes!" Madison huffed. "But that tramp filling in for Winter didn't show up this morning. I had to leave a voice mail message just to fire her. If she can't actually come in and do the work, I refuse to pay her to come in and pick up on her latest target."

Biting her tongue, Raleigh set the cookie trays down amongst the garland and poinsettias decorating the table. Reminding her sister about her own past antics would not be beneficial to Sheri's wedding.

"Of course, I now need to find someone to work the holiday," Madison continued, not paying attention to Raleigh. "Who wants to work at this time of the year? I have three weddings and four New Year's Eve parties. I don't know what I'm going to do."

"Call Reggie," Raleigh said. She scanned the room's festive décor with its circle tables draped in pressed white tablecloths, maroon candles, and mistletoe wrapped in a circle around the center. Gold fabric draped around the back of the chairs tied neatly in a bow completed the look. Eliza had a taste for parties —or the holiday.

With the décor for the parties, Raleigh couldn't tell.

"Reggie Bagert?" Madison asked confused. "Like felony Reggie?"

"He works at the bakery," Raleigh continued. "Being your assistant would be a step up for him."

Even though Madison didn't make good hiring decisions, she did pay well. She tended to hire from her inner circle which often led to disaster. Raleigh could only hope she learned her lesson eventually.

"Reggie won't pass a background check," Madison said, grimacing.

"Your background's not spotless," Raleigh said. "Neither's Winter's."

Winter Spur typically worked for Madison on a regular basis, but the free spirit had recently checked herself into rehab. After getting into a serious relationship where discussions of babies and marriage had come up—brought on by a pregnancy scare, of course, Madison's best friend had become self-reflective. Apparently, the reflection had terrified her enough to make a few changes. She should be home in about two weeks.

Madison glared at her. "Dammit, Raleigh, I hate when you are right. I wonder if he'd start today or at least for Sheri's wedding? I hired staff, but I really need an assistant if I want to enjoy five minutes of this wedding."

"Call him." Raleigh aimed the advice in her sister's direction before going in search of Sheri.

Even though Raleigh had seen the manor from a distance her entire life, she had not stepped foot inside its halls until this past week with Sheri's temporary residency. Although the décor felt stiff and outdated, the home had a warmness to it that Raleigh thought was likely attributed to Eliza. Still, Sheri probably couldn't wait to return to her own home which had currently become the bachelor house. Jeff had decided that in lieu of a bachelor party they'd have a bachelor week. So, Mike had packed a bag and checked in to the debauchery. On the phone last night, he told Raleigh that he was ready for the endless fun to cease. Raleigh could only laugh. Between the dog, the ghosts, and the parties, she hadn't experienced the quiet she thought she would.

Upstairs, Raleigh paused before knocking on Sheri's door and crossed the hall to Claudette's bedroom instead. Pushing the door open, she found Claudette sitting at the dressing table dangling her stocking feet from the upholstered bench.

A soft whimper from a bassinette in the far corner drew Raleigh's attention, and she had to pull her eyes back toward Claudette.

The girl studied Raleigh with mild interest.

"I know what happened to you," Raleigh said.

Claudette's amber eyes flashed. "How come you see me? No one else does."

Stepping inside, Raleigh noticed pale purple walls, twin mahogany canopy beds, twelve-foot ceilings with crown molding, and that strange frilly bassinette in the corner. It's as if they'd created a room for all the girls of the family. "I'm traiteur to the dead. A healer."

"Like you heal the dead? Bring them back to life?" She asked, her tone shifting for the first time.

Raleigh sighed, feeling the impending disappointment. "Not life, but peace. Move on if they want."

Claudette whipped around her face as she turned back toward the mirror. "That's stupid. I don't want peace. I want to live again."

Even though Raleigh had inherited this ability, she had to agree with the child ghost.

Instead, Raleigh said, "Where's the other girl that was with you yesterday?"

Claudette shrugged, not looking at her. "She has a difficult time staying here. This wasn't her home."

Raleigh considered the logistics of Aunt Clarice's comings and goings. The great aunt that wouldn't vacate her residence was tied to her house no matter how crowded the home became. Raleigh assumed she had years of snarky visits to look forward to from the woman who had thoroughly enjoyed her twenties and loved to take that form as a ghost, even though Raleigh had not been born for those years.

"But you must like having her company though?" Raleigh commented, feeling as though she needed to engage to get a read on the girl. To help Sheri, she'd at least have to eliminate the child as a vengeful spirit.

"I have my mama," Claudette said, her words biting. "Still, the girl can be fun. I had to grow up with three brothers who could be quite spiteful."

"Little sisters can be too," Raleigh added, watching her.

Claudette smiled, but it never reached her solemn eyes. "We learn at the hand of our older siblings."

The door across the hall creaked open. "Who are you talking to?" Sheri asked.

Raleigh tore her attention away from Claudette and watched Sheri pad out barefoot in an ivory skirt suit. Besides from the blue eye shadow, not a hint of Sheri's style appeared visible in her wedding ensemble. Raleigh worried that her friend had gone too far in trying to be accepted by the Dantin family. Everyone knew Sheri's outrageous style in obnoxious patterns and bold colors. Raleigh didn't think she'd ever have occasion to miss it. "If you really must know, the girls of the family haven't really left the house," Raleigh said.

Back inside the girl's room, Claudette had disappeared.

"You're kidding, right?" Sheri asked. Fear seized her face.

"Do you need me to be?" Raleigh realized she probably

should have kept that fact to herself longer. At least until she'd figured out how Claudette may or may not be contributing to the issue.

"I can't... I can't..." Sheri began to hyperventilate. "I can't have my baby be a ghost."

Raleigh rushed forward, gripping Sheri's shoulders. "She won't be, I promise."

"You don't know that," Sheri wailed.

"I do," Raleigh said, nodding her head slowly. "Aunt Clarice is helping me now. You know that woman won't stop."

"She is?" Sheri asked, her breathing slowing some from its staccato pace.

Raleigh nodded. "She says she's on a mission to help you, but right now I need you to calm down. I don't know much about babies, but I do know we don't want it to be born high strung from your anxiety."

Sheri released a sharp, nearly hysterical burst of laughter even as a tear slid down her cheek. "I can't sleep here anymore. It's just creepy knowing that they are here. Shawn and I will spend tonight at my mom's. He can have Christmas with his grandparents like he probably wants anyway. The woman's a better Maw than she ever was a mother."

"That's a plan. And tomorrow night, we will have girl's night at my house just like we planned," Raleigh said, wiping some of the tears away. "Everything will work out."

Sheri peered into the empty room. "I just need to explain it to Eliza. Do you think she knows?"

Raleigh considered the set-up of the room. It was as if someone had created a room for three girls, but the girls had all lived at different times. "Maybe, but don't worry about Eliza. It's Christmas Eve. She'll understand you want to be with your family."

Sheri sighed. "I don't though. You have all those Cheramies

who actually like each other, so you don't understand," Sheri scolded. "Have you met my family? Mom will probably have a crisis by 10 AM."

"Well, you and Shawn are welcome to join us Cheramies. With all the people, two more will go unnoticed. Besides I don't think Mike will make it this year. His mother has become jealous of all the time he's spent with the Cheramies and has asked that he spend Christmas with the Simmons this year."

Sheri straightened her suit out and fussed at her auburn hair, even as she focused on taking even breaths. "If I know Mike, he'll find a way not to miss Me'Maw's gumbo or that roast. Besides, the man would prefer to be a Cheramie."

"Hence his mama's jealousy." Raleigh laughed. "Come on now. Let's go have tea like the fancy folk."

"You think I could put a shot of bourbon in it?"

Raleigh feigned mock shock. "Now what would that do to the baby?"

Sheri laughed. "She'd likely turn out just like me. Family joke for years has been that my mama didn't stop sipping from the whisky bottle even during her pregnancies. A little nip here and there and what did Daddy know? He was too busy sneaking off with the neighbor Darlene, who I now have to call step mama."

Raleigh laughed and led Sheri down the stairs.

The chances of this wedding going smoothly between the family drama, a child ghost, and a supposed family curse felt as good as her chances of being a Pulitzer Prize writer working at the Barbeaux Gazette.

Raleigh had her work cut out for her as maid of honor. The job should have come with hazard pay.

CHAPTER FOUR

Raleigh bit into the cucumber sandwich to avoid commenting on the conversation about wedding guest etiquette. With her southern upbringing, she was sure that somewhere in her inner depths she could summon an opinion on the merits of a sit-down dinner versus a buffet, but she didn't think her ideas on a Twix dessert table would go over well with this seven-course meal crowd. She was also having difficulty following the conversation, due to the distraction of the two ghost girls running around the tables, giggling, and playing chase. Of course, no one else noticed their antics. The women were too busy discussing wedding colors and flower coordination.

Claudette and her friend had run through the room during the initial seating and serving line. As the guests waited in line, the two girls oohed and ahhed over the cookie platters, pointing to the various shapes. Putting their faces over the great silver server, they'd smelled the broccoli soup and grimaced. As the old housekeeper and Madison served tea, the two danced around the guests. They'd stared into the attendee's cups, which had ended with a vivacious game of tag. During this race around the tables, the two had nearly collided with guests who socialized as they stood near the buffet and the tables. Raleigh had watched mesmerized by their movement to see what would happen if they touched a person, but she never got a glimpse of it.

"Raleigh," Eliza asked, "what are your thoughts on an outside wedding in December?"

Eliza's sharp eyes fell upon her as the woman set her rose patterned teacup down.

Swallowing the bite she'd taken against the lump that had formed suddenly in her throat, Raleigh wiped her mouth with the holly red napkin. "I think as the bride, Sheri's entitled to whatever kind of wedding she wants. Don't they say something about weddings being every girl's dream?"

Eliza chuckled, the creases on her forehead not moving. "I highly doubt you or Sheri's childhood dreams included weddings since neither of you seemed in a rush to walk down the aisle as most young ladies in our area. I do rather agree with you though. My sons are of the opposite opinion; however. Not that it matters, mind you. We women tend to get what we want."

Jo Ellen Dantin, Jeff's stepmom, had stepped over to their center table with a compliment on Sheri's outfit and had stayed to listen to the conversation. Eliza had handled the seating chart and had placed all the mothers at a table together, just not at the bride's, with her own self at the bridal table, of course. Jo Ellen now regarded the host leerily. "My husband simply worries about the rain. The gardens will be a disaster if the weather is poor."

During the last two weeks they had experienced blue, sunny skies. In fact, Raleigh predicted short pants as the Christmas wardrobe of choice for the holiday. And even though she hadn't checked any recent weather reports, she doubted storm clouds would materialize, at least not within the next forty-eight hours.

The weather had been a source of dissension throughout the wedding, and Sheri had faced much contention over her choice of venue. Three months ago, they'd announced their engagement without a wedding date attached to it. Then at Thanksgiving dinner, they'd announced a Christmas wedding, sending the families into a frenzy. The outside location had been the tipping point.

Eliza winked at Sheri. "A good planner always has Plan B, but Plan A is a go until everything fails."

Jo Ellen frowned but didn't resuscitate the argument. She patted Sheri on the shoulder and returned to her seat.

Eliza folded her hands on the tablecloth in front of her. "I had a church wedding. My catholic parents offered no other options for the matter, but Alfredo and I renewed our vows under the oak tree for our tenth anniversary. Our two eldest boys were young, and we wanted to celebrate our new home."

As she spoke, Claudette gravitated toward her side. The girl's curls spilled across Eliza's shoulder as she placed her chin right up to her shoulder. The other girl tugged on Claudette's arm, but the ghost daughter ignored her playmate.

Raleigh forced herself to focus on the conversation. "What happened to that oak tree?"

She'd seen it during the memory of the past, but at the engagement party last night, it had clearly not been lit up with all the landscape lighting.

Claudette glared at Raleigh, but Raleigh forced herself to focus on Eliza.

Eliza's face folded in on itself like an accordion. "We had it chopped down after the accident. I couldn't bare the sight of it. Hopefully with this new marriage, the possibility of a girl running around these old halls can return some of the joy this house used to contain."

Claudette's face darkened and she glared at her mother now.

Unaware of her daughter's feelings on the matter, Eliza continued, "Have you and Jeff spoke about having a family, dear? I'm sure your son would love a sibling or two."

Sheri laughed, her nervous energy distracting Claudette.

"We have talked about it." Sheri's eyes darted toward Raleigh. "Maybe soon."

Sheri nibbled on her cookie, but her expression remained one of alarm. She wouldn't keep a secret long if these questions continued.

Raleigh stepped in. "Let's not pressure them yet. I'm already struggling to keep up with the life goals of a thirty year old."

Eliza laughed and opened her mouth to say something, but Horace breezed in, throwing an airy compliment at the housekeeper.

Eliza turned toward her son grimacing at him as he approached. Claudette glared at him, moving in closer to her mother. Again, Raleigh wondered if the accident had been intentional.

"Are you party crashing now, son?" Eliza uttered, a tone of distaste. "I raised you better."

"Relax mother. You can have your little soiree." Horace said, shaking his head of salt and pepper hair. "I'm here because a present from Mathis has been delivered, and I have come to ask where you would have me send it."

Horace darted a quick glance at Sheri, but he focused his attention on his mother, designating her as the important person in the room.

"Ah, my errant brother," Eliza said, offering the table a mischievous smile. "He remains bitter after all these years.

Since he didn't inherit the manor from our daddy, he only visits for special occasions."

Horace cleared his throat. "It does sting not to be loved by one's parents."

"Inheritance does not equal love," Eliza responded sharply. "Place Mathis's gift in Sheri's bedroom. Jeff can retrieve it along with the others to bring it to that lovely new home of theirs."

"Uncle Mathis did RSVP to the wedding," Sheri said. "Do you believe he will not attend?"

Eliza tssked. "Of course, he will attend. What could be more special than a Dantin wedding? He sent the gift to remind me of his grudge, even though he has made a good life for himself in the city."

"I must say," Raleigh said, avoiding the gloomy expression of Claudette, "a woman inheriting over a brother at your time wasn't the popular choice."

Eliza chuckled, leaning back in her chair. "I had four brothers, each a scoundrel in their own right. Mathis became successful only because Daddy disinherited him after a round of bad decisions. My eldest brother died in a duel by the hands of my hothead younger brother, which caused Elmire to drink himself to death within a year. And then Hinkle, ah Hinkle decided to get on a ship and never return. We assumed he was lost at sea, but he could show up any day with tales to tell."

"So, you were the smart choice?" Raleigh said.

Eliza grinned. "I provided the continuation of the family line, and my father appreciated my husband's last name being the same as my own. Yes, I know the questions that must raise, but we were not relatives that we could trace."

Eliza smiled at Sheri, endearment in her expression.

Sheri had clearly won Eliza over already. Having a girl would seal the old woman's love forever. The other Dantins required something more for them to like her, and Sheri seemed to be stripping her personality down to make it happen.

Claudette moved closer and closer to her mother until she touched her cheek against her mother's chest.

Eliza shivered under the contact and pulled the shawl draped over her shoulders tighter around her chest. "This old manor's always giving me chills."

Raleigh suspected what had aged along with the manor was Claudette's spirit and fifty years had strengthened the girl's presence. Her mother felt her even if she couldn't see her.

The question remained though. Had Claudette been responsible for any of the deaths to the girls in this family? Had she wanted company in the in-between?

Raleigh would need to find out soon. She had two days.

CHAPTER FIVE

As Raleigh unrolled silver and blue wrapping paper across the rug, Mike entered the living room carrying an oversized tray of food. He grabbed a slice of baked honey ham, set the tray down, and sank onto the sofa across from her position on the floor, opposite the sleeping dog. Raleigh continued wrapping the large square box. As in her yearly Christmas tradition, she'd delayed wrapping the presents until the last minute.

Through garbled words, Mike spoke as he chewed on the ham that Me'Maw had sent over for them. "I'm glad Jeff paused the wedding shenanigans for Christmas. Our first year dating, and we didn't get to start any traditions. Like cookies or eggnog."

Food. The way to her man's heart most certainly was food.

Raleigh struggled with the wrapping paper, and it ripped at the corner of the remote-control plane her nephew Mason wanted for Christmas. "I hope the spirits aren't one of our new Christmas traditions. Children spirits make the holiday especially gloomy."

Lowering himself to the floor, Mike grabbed the plush bathrobe she'd bought Madison at a department store sale. Raleigh had been sure to get a gift receipt as her sister tended to return everything and put the money toward some high-end purchase she deemed worthy. He said, "I'm sorry I haven't been any help. Jeff hasn't said anything, and I don't want to be the one who informs him that there's a ghost situation."

Raleigh tossed the crumpled paper aside and leaned back against the over-stuffed chair. "I don't know if he knows anything. I do think it strange about the bedroom situation that makes me wonder if Eliza knows something. But then she can't, right?"

Raleigh felt like there should be some kind of ghost communicator support group, especially if there was more than one of her on the bayou. There should be somewhere to go and commiserate with others on the struggle of the dying commandeering your life—in Raleigh's case that could be literal take over.

"I've never known anyone besides you to talk to the dead." Mike stretched out towards her, moving along the floor. "Jeff and I met in kindergarten, and he never mentioned a sister. I'd imagine she'd be older than him, right?"

Raleigh thought about Claudette's playmate. The blonde girl with the delicate features had appeared to be around the same age as Claudette, but her presence hadn't been as strong. Raleigh suspected that this second child had been Jeff's sister, but she'd need to confirm. At this point, Claudette could have picked up a stranger in the cemetery and brought her home to play. Perhaps Aunt Clarice could offer guidance on the logistics of how hauntings worked. Raleigh usually only dealt with residual spiritual energy as it left the body.

Aunt Clarice had never volunteered any information before though. Likely because she didn't want Raleigh to evict her. She didn't need to go in search of Aunt Clarice's answers tonight though, even with this impending sense of urgency over Sheri's situation. Aunt Clarice's visits still freaked Mike out, and Aunt

Clarice had decided to adapt him to their living arrangement at a slower pace. The errant woman had promised not to show up randomly when he was around.

Raleigh gazed out at the Christmas tree with its hand-me-down ornaments from her Me'Maw—some likely older than her. She preferred her possessions this way. All hand-me-down items from her older family members that came with a story. All the decorative items in her house had been passed down through Aunt Clarice's travels, and lucky for her (or unlucky), the woman could still drop in and tell her a tale about how they'd been acquired. She had imagined her vacation being about wedding and Christmas bells though, not about children and pesky great aunt spirits.

Moving over, Raleigh fit herself under the crook of Mike's arm. "How about we have a good Christmas Eve instead of all this talk of ghosts. I'll wrap the presents tomorrow morning before I walk over to Me'Maw's and Paw's."

Mike kissed the top of the head and snuggled in closer.

With a loud head shake, Luna rose from her sleeping position on the sofa, stretched out on her hind legs, and slid down, head butting them with her pointed lab nose. She'd waited until they'd gotten close to assert her presence, as usual.

The two laughed and allowed her to climb into their lap which lasted all of three seconds before she discovered the crinkle of the wrapping paper on the floor. Then she began swatting at the shiny paper while Raleigh and Mike took the opportunity to snack on the food Me'Maw had sent over. Raleigh really didn't need anything more than this in terms of Christmas traditions. This felt perfect.

Later in the evening, she and Mike had finally settled Luna down in her flannel doggy bed, and while trying to go to sleep, Raleigh listened to Mike's deep breathing and Luna's snoring. The holiday usually brought a level of excitement, and the wedding and impending possibility of trouble had only amped this up. One minute she'd been listening to the sounds of sleep around her and the next she felt herself waking up to a familiar tapping.

As she sat up in bed, Mike mumbled in his sleep. Raleigh hurried and slid out her side of the bed without waking him. Her lovely patient boyfriend had barely recovered from the one incident he'd seen a ghost in the living room—Aunt Clarice's shenanigans. Raleigh didn't want to ruin Christmas.

Downstairs, the incorrigible houseguest stood pursed at the front door mid-knock.

Aunt Clarice jutted a hip out, smiled, and propped her right hand high with her dangling Virginia Slim.

"Are you ready for our mission, Dearie?" the woman asked. With her hair in a short bob and a purple linen pant suit, this was the older version that Raleigh remembered. The woman from her childhood—the Great Aunt she'd found fascinating with all the knick-knacks from all over the world. They'd somewhat lost their shine now that Raleigh had to dust them.

"Our mission isn't complete?" Raleigh asked. "Exactly how many of these middle of the night trips do we have?"

Aunt Clarice grinned, her head twitching. "A standard three-night visitation to the past, the past, and the future."

Aunt Clarice had been reading too many Christmas stories instead of her fashion magazines.

Raleigh grumbled, "Didn't scrooge get the past, present, and future?"

Aunt Clarice's coarse hearty laugh echoed in the silent house. "Hun, you are no scrooge. Maybe a Carrie. You don't need a glimpse at the present with your ability to see the ghosts of two little mischievous spirits. You just need a little help with the other two."

For the record, Raleigh had never gone crazy at prom and

murdered people like Stephen King's Carrie, although she had been responsible for the death of one of the most popular football players. He'd tried to kill her first though. Prom had been a miserable affair after this ordeal and Carrie's abilities would have come in handy.

Raleigh didn't need to debate this right now with her cheeky aunt though. Groaning, she touched Aunt Clarice's shimmering hand.

A moment of blackness descended, and Raleigh blinked. When she opened them, she stood at the top of the mahogany staircase of Dantin Manor.

Looking around, Raleigh searched for some hint as to what time in the past they'd come to visit on their journey. The deep navy wallpaper appeared the same as it had during this week's wedding festivities. She remembered seeing many of the family portraits from passing them in the halls on her way up and down. She didn't see Jeff's family portrait so that offered some semblance of a time frame.

In a burst of energy, an abundantly pregnant woman emerged from the far-left bedroom. She hurried forward, tears still trailing down her pale, puffy face.

A younger Horace with wavy, dark hair followed behind her a moment later. "You can't leave, Eleanor. You're just feeling rash because of the hormones. Come back and calm down so we can discuss this."

Eleanor pivoted, rage gripping her face, clenching her fists. "We should both be leaving! We should be making a family home."

"But this is my home," Horace pleaded.

"It's not *our* home," Eleanor emphasized. "You will never grow up, make your own decisions, or be a man of your own if you don't get out of this house!"

Crossing his arms across his chest, Horace scowled. "I'm not leaving. It has always been my dream to live and raise my family here. You knew this about me."

Eleanor threw up her hands. "Fine! You can have the house but not your family! I hope it makes you happy."

As she spun around, the heaviness of her belly tipped her forward, throwing her off-balance. She stumbled, one foot stubbing against the other. She flailed, grasping at the air.

It felt as if the horrific scene dragged on, stalling before Raleigh. Horace stood feet away.

Claudette shimmered between them. "Save her."

Horace's complexion paled, and he froze, staring at his sister.

Eleanor tumbled down the stairs, her belly hitting the third step first before more thuds ensued.

Raleigh closed her eyes to the horrible sounds.

When she opened them, Horace remained standing at the foot of the stairs blinking, unmoving. For a moment, his expression appeared one of vindictive pleasure. Then terror crept in as her unmoving form registered.

Raleigh looked toward Aunt Clarice, unable to watch this horror any longer.

"I believe you know what happened to the baby," Aunt Clarice said, her face grim.

"What about Eleanor?" Raleigh whispered as if Horace could hear them.

Aunt Clarice tilted her head. She'd lost her cigarette, but she looked as though she wanted one. "She healed but refused to return to this house. Several years later she remarried. I believe she has four children and three grandchildren now."

Raleigh grimaced. She still didn't see a curse in action though. Without a looking glass into Horace's mind, both could have been accidents. Although he did seem to have a predictable behavior in an emergency—not someone you'd want around. She must be missing something in the details. She didn't know what though.

With a chilling touch of Aunt Clarice's hand, everything went black again. She blinked and when she opened her eyes the sunlight blinded her. She blinked repeatedly, trying to focus on the party happening around the pool.

A cluster of three teenagers floated in bright orange rafts in the pool, crisp skin and dark shades adding to their looks of noninterest. Near a makeshift cabana a group of six adults lounged in chairs. Music blared from a stereo system reminiscent of those popular in the 80s, another hint as to where she was in the past. None of the adults appeared to be supervising the children running around the pool.

A lanky man with a head full of dark hair, a construction tan, and too small swim trunks manned a grill near the edge of the back corner. Raleigh had only seen Jeff's father a half dozen times, but she'd say with certainty that this was Alcee Dantin, albeit a younger version than the one who'd come to watch Jeff's basketball games in high school.

A shriek jarred through Raleigh's spine, and she returned her attention to the crowd under the blue umbrella. With a flimsy bathrobe tied loosely around his swim trunks, Horace sprayed champagne from a bottle. From thinning hair and softening jowl, she could assume a few years had passed from the last memory they'd walked through.

Through the spray, a small boy streaked by, tiny feet carrying him across the concrete decking as a slightly older girl chased after him. The boy had one floatie on and the girl gripped the other one in her hands. As the girl ran in front of Raleigh, she recognized the blonde that was Claudette's playmate. The one Claudette had said didn't live in Dantin Manor.

The boy weaved in and out of the inebriated adults without

any of them as much as glancing his way before skidding to a stop at the man at the grill.

"Daddy," he shrilled. "Can I go in the deep end?"

Alcee Dantin turned from the grill and surveyed the situation. Raleigh couldn't read his thoughts, but she assumed his matched her own about the responsibility of the current adults. "Only if you let Rebecca put that floatie on and she agrees to watch you, Jeff."

Raleigh's heart began to pound. Jeff couldn't be more than three years old. He wouldn't remember having a sister if she'd been taken from him this young. Mason couldn't remember where he put his cheese puff's bag down five minutes ago, and he was six years old now.

Jeff glanced back at Rebecca and scowled. "I hate the floaties. They itch me."

"Then you will have to stay on the shallow side," Alcee said, studying him sternly. To Rebecca he said, "I need you to keep an eye on him today."

Rebecca pouted. "Why do I always have to watch him?"

Alcee looked over at the merry group of adults tracing letters on each other's backs and guessing like some middle school game. "I tell you what, you do this for me today, and I will let you have a sleepover with your friends this weekend."

Rebecca grumbled, her body slumping. "You better not change your mind again."

Alcee sighed, returning to flip the burgers as a flame shot up from the coals.

Jeff sprinted toward the far side of the pool where the teenagers lazed on rafts, seemingly asleep as no movement had come from them since Raleigh had stood watching.

Raleigh watched Rebecca struggle with a wiggly Jeff to put the remaining floatie on his arm. She dipped it in water. She yanked and pulled and shimmied but the floatie would not slide up his arm. Her face gritted in determination and eventually frustration.

Jeff grew impatient and wigglier, until he twisted away from her yelling. "I use one floatie."

She tried to grab at him, but he jumped in the pool. The propulsion forced his floatie to pop off and land within feet of his head. His face registered surprise only for a moment before he began to sink.

Rebecca jumped in immediately. All arms and legs, Rebecca appeared not much larger than the solidly built Jeff. She struggled to keep the two of them afloat. Jeff swallowed water as Rebecca couldn't keep his head above water and both of them afloat. Jeff's arms swung out in desperation, colliding with Rebecca's face even as she struggled to kick them to the surface.

She swallowed water and choked against the inhale. She slipped under water as she fought to keep Jeff's head from submerging.

Someone in the crowd of adults laughed as Raleigh looked on horrified. No one glanced toward the pool.

Rebecca resurfaced and Raleigh saw resignation in the child's eyes.

She wouldn't be able to save both of them. And she'd known it in that moment. At seven years old she'd understood her own exhaustion and that she wouldn't make it. The struggle had depleted her.

Rebecca struggled to choke out words to Jeff even as she swallowed water. Raleigh couldn't hear them, but Jeff nodded and some of his panicky struggle slowed. With an effort that separated the two, Rebecca heaved Jeff toward the side of the pool.

Jeff's hands reached out for the ledge and his fingertips brushed against it. Panic seized him though, and he flailed his arms in a last-ditch effort to save himself. It offered just enough for him to reach the edge and cling to the side with his face just above water.

Rebecca never resurfaced. A dark shadow now appeared at the bottom of the pool.

Claudette appeared near the grill a few feet from Alcee.

The man had looked longingly toward the group enjoying the day, but his eyes met Claudette's instead. He froze.

"Save her."

He blinked rapidly against the shimmery mirage before him.

"Save her," Claudette insisted

One of the partiers shrieked, causing Alcee to breathe again.

Alcee dropped the spatula with a clang to the cement and sprinted toward the deep end. Yanking Jeff out of the water by his forearm, he clung to his son even as Jeff sputtered against his chest, struggling to fill his lungs with air.

A blonde woman tore herself from the group and jogged over, trying to take Jeff from Alcee. "Why was he on this side of the pool? You were supposed to be watching him today!"

Alcee pulled Jeff away from his chest and examined him. "I asked Rebecca to put his floaties on and watch him. I can't cook and watch the kids at the same time. You should be helping."

"So, this is my fault?" she said shrilly, pulling at Jeff still. Jeff clung to his father's big arms though and buried his head in his chest. "Where's Rebecca? You know you can't trust that girl to watch him. Her head's always in the clouds. Why would you even ask her to do something so important?"

Another shriek pierced through the bickering. This time one of the teenagers from the raft. The commotion had lulled them from their sunbathing coma, and one of them had registered Rebecca lying at the bottom of the pool.

If Jeff had any memories of this day, he'd have been in costly therapy for his entire life. Sometimes forgetting had benefits.

Aunt Clarice looked to Raleigh, her face grimacing with pain. "And we know how this one ends as well."

Besides from the cameo appearance of Claudette, this had been a horrible tragedy. At least as far as Raleigh could see. Horrible parenting, yes, but tragedy none the less.

Raleigh looked at Aunt Clarice's outstretched arm, ready to take her back to the present. "Do spirits become more concrete as they age? Can they choose who they show themselves to?"

Aunt Clarice inhaled as she appeared to consider the questions. "The area's muddy—complicated. They can become stronger the longer they are here and cling to people. They draw on their energy, you see. But you know that people must be open to seeing. They must believe. I'd say Claudette is haunting this family."

Raleigh nodded, slowly. Considering this.

Claudette was haunting her family, and Raleigh suspected they knew it. They'd been surprised, but they'd seen her.

On the other hand, Claudette had said "save her" both times. That didn't feel malicious. So, what exactly did the child spirit want?

And even with all of that, Raleigh still didn't know how she could stop Sheri's daughter being the fourth Dantin girl spirit taken from the living.

CHAPTER SIX

In the morning, she woke again having no recollection of how she'd returned to bed. Mike swore he hadn't felt her stir all night, but the man had slept through his house burning so she didn't know how much his word meant in this situation. It did mean that she had no certainty that the whole incident had not been some vivid dream.

Dream or not didn't matter though. She'd learned how the three Dantin girls died, but she had no idea how that knowledge would help Sheri.

If Horace had been a clear suspect, she could find a witness or evidence to eliminate him as a threat. Or if Claudette served as a threat because she'd taken to some vindictive haunting, Raleigh could work on that with her own methods.

Neither had emerged as a clear culprit though.

She felt no closer to figuring it out than she had two days ago.

What she didn't have to puzzle over and drive herself crazy with was Christmas with her family.

Aunt Mabel brought the tarte a la bouille, and Aunt Vera said their mama's had been better. Cousin Jolie soothed their argument by asking about their grandchildren who'd moved to Oklahoma. Father Lucas blessed the food with a prayer, and Me'Maw stood regal beside him, proud of her two days of preparation. The tables and plates were ladened down by the baked ham, the roast, gumbo, rice dressing, the stuffed mirliton, the fried okra, and so many other vegetables that Paw had harvested in preparation. Everyone filled a plate and perched wherever they found an empty spot in the house full of extended family.

Since Raleigh did not have a child to chase after nor a significant other to entertain, she garnered kitchen duty. Although the Formica countertops were loaded down buffet style, someone always needed help with serving spoons or condiments. Sometimes job duties included cleaning up a cup of red pop rouge on the yellow linoleum floor. Raleigh didn't complain when her mom and Aunt didn't help because it would be Me'Maw who would come to her aid. And her grandmother appeared exhausted from the holiday preparations. Instead, she watched Me'Maw settle into her favorite spot on the warm tan sofa and brought the woman a small plate of food, otherwise she wouldn't eat after all that work. Still, she barely grazed the food as she conversed in Cajun French with her sister. Raleigh only caught a few words like "tete deur," and "maquereau." Raleigh didn't even want to know who they were calling a hardheaded womanizer.

Raleigh had never gone in for the gossip anyway, except when she needed to scour it for information on the latest murder. But her family would unlikely have any intimate details on the Dantin family as Eliza's family belonged to old Barbeaux royalty, the haves, and the Cheramies were more of the peasants, the have nots. The sides didn't really run in the same circles, even in gossip circles.

After Uncle Jude filled his plate for the second time,

Raleigh excused herself from her duties, ducking out the back screen door with a plate of food. With all the ruckus in the house, she needed five minutes in her own favorite spot before she began clean up patrol.

Her back porch haven was occupied though.

With his legs hanging over the edge of the plank porch boards, Paw stared out over the garden with Luna sprawled out next to him.

"Dammit," Raleigh said, "Did she get out again?"

Luna had taken to digging a hole under the back picket fence to visit Paw on a near daily basis. Mike repaired hole after hole, but it did not deter her afternoon jaunts down the street to Me'Maw and Paw's backyard where she nudged at the screen door with her nose if Paw happened to be inside. She and Mike had discussed changing out the fence for one that extended beneath the ground a few inches, but they hesitated at the expense, certain that Luna would find another way to visit her favorite person. The one who kept treats in one pocket for himself—peanuts—and the other pocket for her—beef jerky.

"I went get her," Paw said sheepishly. "She shouldn't spend Christmas alone."

Raleigh shook her head, smiling. "You aren't helping."

Paw shrugged, his jaw set. "Raleigh Lynn, I'm an old man. I can spoil my great-granddog."

Raleigh laughed. Smelling food, Luna lumbered up and heeled in front of Raleigh. Tossing her a piece of Christmas ham, Raleigh eased herself next to Paw, dangling her legs off the back porch.

Paw tossed a peanut shell into the grass. "So, what has you out here by yourself?"

"I just needed a minute," Raleigh said, inhaling the fresh air. The house had become stuffy about ten guests or so ago. "Love the family but they can kick up some noise."

Paw nodded, his usual somber expression firmly intact. "That you right, but I can see you have something on your mind, Raleigh Lynn. So have at it. What trouble you getting up to now?"

Paw called the business of helping the dead trouble. He didn't mean anything by it as Paw approved of the helping. Years before, when he'd believed she'd been more meddlesome than altruistic, he'd heartedly disapproved and expressed it by attempting the silent treatment with only the occasional commentary.

The two stared out over the rows in the garden where cabbage and lettuce had not succumbed to a freeze yet, which would likely come in January. Only a day or two of cold weather this year was predicted, so it would be possible the late blooming cabbage would survive and not brown around the edges if Paw didn't pick them all to trade or sell.

"Sheri needs my help," Raleigh said, glancing over at Paw who sat statuesque looking out over his garden. "I can't figure out why the girls in Jeff's family die. There seems to be no consistency in the causes."

"Hmm," Paw said, fiddling with a peanut shell between his thumb and forefinger. "And I suppose Sheri's going to have a girl?"

Raleigh looked over at him surprised. "How did you know Sheri was going to have a baby?"

Paw chuckled, tossing the shell into the grass. "Raleigh Lynn, you aren't the only one with family talents. Your Me'Maw began quilting a pink blanket last week, certain it was a girl. I thought she might be wrong for the first time being Jeff's family's all boys, but with what you say, it makes sense now."

"Did you ever hear anything about the family?" Raleigh asked. "You usually know all the important news."

Paw's jaw deepened into a scowl. He hated gossip, believed

it to be the language of spite. But through his once-a-week breakfasts down at the diner and the steady customers cleaning shoes on the doormat, Paw knew most of what went on around Barbeaux, at least with the over forty crowd.

"Alcee bought the old Adeax farm about the time you were in kindergarten. Only reason I remember is because he asked for advice on tractors, and you came out there with me right after I got you off the school bus." Paw frowned again. She could tell he was branching out into uncomfortable territory. "Alcee had no farming skills, but it seemed as though he'd had a falling out with the entire Dantin clan. That wife of his had up and run off with some guitar player from a New Orleans bar, and he was raising Jeff by himself. He seemed content with it all every time I changed a part out on that old bum tractor. He married Jo Ellen a year later and Me'Maw pieced them a quilt."

Jeff's stepmom had raised him, and he'd never expressed an issue with her. Jo Ellen had two sons and a daughter from a previous marriage, so Alcee and Joe Ellen had considered the family complete. Mike had helped Nate, Jeff, and Samuel bale hay, feed cows, and mend fences most of their teenage years. Raleigh and Mike worked down at the Barbeaux Gazette together, but Mike still helped on weekends sometimes with the brothers. Samuel, the oldest stepbrother, was the only one left working full time on the farm with his dad. Nate and Jeff had both ventured into construction, which Mike had been known to help out on a crew when needed as well. Mike had always been wrapped up with these men, and they'd never spoken about a dead sister.

"The girls haunt Dantin manor," Raleigh said. "I don't like the spirits of children. Quite depressing at Christmas."

Paw's big hand gently patted her leg. "Don't think of the bad. Just imagine how you can help. Best advice Me'Maw has to offer."

Raleigh sighed, feeling useless in the help department. "It can't be easy living with their strong presence."

Paw picked up a piece of turkey from Raleigh's plate and tossed it to Luna. "Sometimes you and Me'Maw forget how terrifying the whole spirit thing can be for a normal person. I'm sure Mike's going through his adjustment period right now, just like I had to do all those years ago. And speak of the man himself."

Glancing back, Raleigh watched Mike emerge through the back screen door with Sheri and Jeff lapping at his heels. Luna excitedly rushed him, placing her paws on his chest as if reaching for a hug. Mike embraced her while offering Raleigh his goofy grin.

"What happened to dinner at your mom's?" Raleigh asked.

"Katie burned the turkey and set the fire alarm off. All of which caused her and mom to start arguing," Mike said, shaking her head. "Someone threw the mashed potatoes. Of course, neither claim credit for the mess that my nephew ended up cleaning up. At the end of the scream fest, they decided to have lunch at Shoney's, and I decided Me'Maw offered a better menu."

Paw chuckled. "Even better company."

Looking past Mike toward Sheri and Jeff, Raleigh asked. "And what about you two?"

Sheri flinched and Jeff squeezed her hand. "Our families decided to have Christmas dinner together this year. You know, with the wedding and all. They didn't exactly throw potatoes, but..."

Jeff shook his head. "It was a terrible idea from the start. Her mom insulted Jo Ellen's casserole or some nonsense like that. No one heard the insult except for my dad. Then they all argued over whose family believed they were better than the other." Jeff grimaced. "We snuck out and left them to figure it out and let us know the answer later."

Mike chuckled. "Don't get me wrong, I love Joe Ellen, but her casserole has always been awful. Remember when we fed it to that old mut under the table?"

Jeff smiled. "Old Reg wouldn't even eat it sometimes. He'd smell it and hide behind the recliner."

Sheri sucked in hard, her face reflecting embarrassment like a broken Christmas ornament. "My mom should know better though. She was awful."

Jeff pulled her closer to his side. Sheri was a tall woman so her head could rest on Jeff's shoulder. "They'll figure it out."

With a heave and cracking of the joints, Paw stood and hobbled toward the back door. "We always have plenty of food here, so you came to the right place. Sometimes families take a while to act right. Sometimes you build your own when they can't seem to get it together. Come inside and fix you some food before Jude eats it all. He's probably on at least his third plate by now."

Opening the screen door, he motioned for the group to enter the kitchen. Luna took that as her invitation and sprinted into the house.

Grinning, Mike shook his head. Paw had owned a dog for fourteen years and the poor thing had never entered the house. Back then Paw insisted that animals belonged outside. Raleigh knew for a fact that Luna spent most of her days curled up at Paw's feet as he rocked in his rocker. Me'Maw said she'd never seen anything like it—tete deur changing his mind. Hard head had certainly grown soft in his old age.

After everyone served themselves heaping plates of food, they returned to the porch haven where the noise decibel didn't reach deafening proportions. Mason and Shawn, Sheri's son, tossed a new football around with Luna running back and forth attempting to intercept.

So that Jeff and Sheri could have a place to sit, Raleigh cleared off the old metal glider that had once belonged to Me'Maw's mother, the one she could thank for her ability to speak to the dead. She and Mike sat at the edge of the porch with their legs dangling over, just as they'd done since they'd been children.

"So, Sheri tells me the Dantin manor is haunted," Jeff said before swallowing a bite of gumbo. "I always knew something was wrong with that big old house and that's why my dad didn't like visiting."

"Your sister drowned there," Raleigh said, setting her bowl of bread pudding down. Aunt Vera had out done herself this year. The bourbon sauce just might cause her to have to walk instead of drive the rest of the day though. The old woman's eyes were probably as bad as she insisted. "I'm sure your sister's death had more to do with his dislike of the house than anything else. Most people don't see ghosts."

"Maybe," Jeff said, spoon paused in the air as he considered it. "But he does believe in ghosts. He's never told any stories about why. It does make you wonder though."

"Have you ever seen a ghost?" Raleigh asked.

"We aren't all like you." Sheri laughed. "I don't want my baby turning into a ghost though."

Jeff looked toward her. "She won't. After this wedding, we can avoid the entire family. My dad says every death happened at that house, so we don't need to return after the wedding."

Sheri exhaled deeply and nodded. The furrow in the middle of her forehead revealed a hint of disbelief still.

"That's true," Raleigh said, more to reassure Sheri than her belief in Jeff's theory. All three had seemed like tragic accidents not necessarily related to the house. Raleigh didn't know about curses, but she might become a believer soon.

The wrinkles in the middle of Sheri's forehead relaxed.

"How would you react if you saw a ghost?" Raleigh asked. The one factor nagging her had been both Horace and Alcee's reaction to Claudette. It felt like an unknown.

Mike chuckled. "We both know I didn't have the best reaction."

Raleigh bumped her shoulder against his. "I think that's pretty normal though for a first time."

Sheri nodded. "I'd be terrified. It just doesn't seem natural, no matter how friendly you assure me Aunt Clarice is."

"I don't know," Jeff said slumping into the rocker. "Dad once told me that as a young boy I used to claim I was playing with Rebecca. He believed I could see her ghost."

Sheri looked startled. "You never told me that."

Jeff shook his head. "It's been a long time since I've even thought about it. I don't really remember having a sister. My memory of her comes only from the few photographs my mother didn't burn after an argument with my dad."

"That's terrible," Sheri said, shuttering.

Raleigh said, "I bet Rebecca's ghost stopped visiting when your mother left."

"Why would you say that?" Jeff asked taken aback.

Because daughters haunted their mothers, especially those who'd had such a terrible reaction when their daughter died.

"Just a hunch," Raleigh said. "I will look into it while you enjoy the wedding festivities."

"Look into it?" Sheri asked alarmed. "You think something's going to happen to my baby?"

"No," Raleigh emphasized. "The facts are though that something has happened to three girls in Jeff's family when a girl is set to inherit the manor. That may or may not be a coincidence, but I can find out."

Jeff wrapped a free arm around Sheri, abandoning his spoon. "We could just refuse the inheritance if that's what causes it. I don't care about some ancient Dantin relic as long as our daughter is safe."

Sheri exhaled, trying to put on a brave face.

Mike paused in shoveling down spoonsful of gumbo. "You have the best two working on it with Raleigh and Aunt Clarice. You two will only need to figure out how to raise a girl. From what I see, it must be difficult."

Raleigh elbowed him. "Not all girls are like Madison and Katie."

The screen door opened, and Madison came out. "What about me?"

Mike laughed as Raleigh squirmed. "We're talking about the difference between raising a girl and raising a boy."

"Ugh," Madison said, leaning against the screen door. "I'm sure girls can't possibly talk about disgusting things all the time. What does that have to do with sisters though?"

Not wanting to start a war on Christmas day, Raleigh said, "Is Me'Maw ready to open presents?"

Madison nodded, her eyes narrowing suspiciously. "That's why I was sent to retrieve you and the kids. Like Mason needs anymore toys today. Mama went overboard as usual."

Raleigh stood. "It wouldn't be a Cheramie Christmas if we didn't have too much food, too much noise, and too many presents. Aren't you glad to be part of this family instead of one not celebrating?"

Madison puzzled over Raleigh's words. "I guess if you want to be part of all this craziness."

Six years and an entire chasm separated Raleigh and her sister, but recent events left Raleigh feeling grateful that she had a sister that wasn't a ghost, even if Madison tended to stir up trouble.

Raleigh laughed. "Merry Christmas Madison. Now let's go add to the mess of toys you'll have to clean up."

Madison groaned but she allowed Raleigh to lead her back into the den of chaos. Mike whistled for Luna and the boys to enter the present frenzy. And all was right with the world for a few hours.

CHAPTER SEVEN

Only a few hours later, Raleigh hid the bottle of sparkling grape juice in her fridge behind a questionable Tupperware container, while handing Sheri a champagne flute with her free hand. Surveying her kitchen's bar top filled with sandwich trays, fruit platters and an interesting cheese tray that Elizabeth, Jeff's step-sister, had brought, Raleigh figured she'd added another room in her home to the growing list that needed to be cleaned. Probably not until after the wedding, but she could pretend it would get done soon while she stood frowning at the clutter.

She picked up her own champagne glass near the sink where she'd left it instead of contemplating her lack of house-keeping skills. "So, you really think you'll be able to keep it quiet much longer?"

Sheri's gaze slid sideways toward the living room where the other bridesmaids were giggling over these mud masks that Raleigh had been gifted from one of the Barbeaux Gazette's ad sponsors. The new downtown shop owner had likely wanted a story featuring her organic skincare essentials, but Raleigh avoided fluff pieces like her editor avoided the Santa suit for the local Christmas festival.

"We have the whole announcement planned out," Sheri whispered. "We have placed cards in everyone's Papa Noel stockings. Our parents will wake up New Year's Day to the news, and we don't even have to be there in person."

The tradition of Papa Noel filling a sock or a shoe on New Year's Eve had been one firmly in place in this small town. It wasn't until Raleigh had lived in Texas for a few years and then later Baton Rouge that she'd realized that most people didn't have two versions of Father Christmas visiting them every year.

"Well, you aren't showing yet, so no one will guess," Raleigh said. "But apparently Me'Maw knows."

Sheri looked down at her form as if looking for a bump, which was only noticeable if you knew what you were looking for. "Your grandmother knows everything. Think she'd be able to tell me if my baby will be safe?"

A chill ran through Raleigh. "Let's give it a day or two before we ask."

As traiteur, Me'Maw offered healing prayers and perhaps creams for arthritis and the like. Even though she didn't advertise or lay claim to it, she could glimpse the future. She didn't like to "read" for people as she called it, said it became a self-fulfilling prophecy that people caused to happen. Raleigh didn't need anything else to cause Sheri to worry, especially if it was something Raleigh couldn't prevent.

When they returned to the living room, Madison had convinced the other two to try these green tea and chamomile foot masks, so Elizabeth and Stephanie were waving their feet in the air and giggling at how weird it felt. The high-pitched screeching was likely attributed to the two bottles of champagne they'd killed. How they'd manage fresh faces and cheery smiles for the wedding tomorrow would be all on them. Raleigh wanted to at least look decent if the photographs would hang on a wall forever.

"Join us!" Stephanie called, jabbing a foot at them. "You should be pampered for your wedding tomorrow."

Completely disregarding the thick green layer on her feet, Stephanie jumped up and rushed upon Sheri, pulling her towards the chair—Aunt Clarice's chair. With eyes wide, Sheri gawked back at Raleigh. Raleigh waved permission, regretting having told anyone that Aunt Clarice spent many evenings lounging in that chair flipping through fashion magazines. No one wanted to sit in her seat now, besides Madison, of course, who didn't care. Her insufferable sister said the blue velvet upholstered chair offered the best seat in the room, and there was no reason to leave it open when Aunt Clarice clearly didn't have a body to enjoy it.

Stephanie tumbled to the floor at Sheri's feet with a giggle. "Just wait until you feel it squishing between your toes."

"I don't know if I want to." Sheri regarded her skeptically. "Besides, I went to the spa a few days ago to prepare for the wedding festivities. I don't need another foot treatment."

"Nonsense," Stephanie said, her voice high-pitched and exaggerated. "A woman can never have too much pampering."

Elizabeth raised a near empty glass. "Or too much champagne!"

Madison leaned in, her long dark hair falling over her shoulder. "Your turn now. These ladies have killed my patience. They have drunk two bottles of champagne by themselves, and my one glass has not been enough to keep up with their incessant chatter."

Since Raleigh had only sipped her own glass and poured Sheri's down the drain to replace it with the grape juice, these two seemed to be having a celebration all of their own.

Sheri hadn't planned on a large wedding party. Even three bridesmaids had been more than she'd wanted. Elizabeth had been an obvious choice as a future in-law and so had Raleigh.

Although she and Sheri had not been close friends in high school, they'd been good friends since Raleigh's return to Barbeaux Bayou a year ago. Stephanie had been the questionable decision.

In high school Sheri and Stephanie had been best friends though. Throughout the wedding festivities, Stephanie had seemed insulted Sheri had asked Raleigh to be the maid of honor. Last week the woman had insisted on hosting the bridal shower where she'd toasted to herself for doing all the work. Raleigh's feelings were not hurt. In fact, she'd told Sheri that she could name Stephanie maid of honor if it were an issue. But Sheri did not feel the same as Stephanie and had commented that the two only visited every six weeks when Stephanie needed her hair colored so she could insist she was a natural strawberry blonde.

A soft knock sounded on the front door, nearly missed over Stephanie's loud screeching laugh. Madison jumped up. "I'll get it."

Raleigh had never seen Madison move quickly for any reason. These two must have found a particular path under her sister's nerves.

Moments later, scowling, Madison returned with Amber Ferly trailing behind her. Raleigh's waif of a neighbor wore a sheer fuzzy pink sweater that stopped just before the waistline of a flowing purple skirt. With the lighting, and the fabric contours, she clearly wore no under garments as usual. The woman either had allergies or a personal affront to wearing such things—Raleigh had not brought herself to ask yet. Clutching an overfilled wicker basket, Amber struggled to keep it hip level with her thin, trembling biceps.

Raleigh could only hope she'd brought a gift for the bride. Anything else would probably be a bad omen.

Rolling her eyes, Madison returned to her seat on the sofa. Amber had tried particularly hard to grow on them, but Raleigh felt a small amount of shame that her attempts had not been successful.

"I thought I'd come and wish the bride congratulations." Amber said, her acorn eyes unfocused, floating around the room. "I thought you might like to do an energy cleanse to wipe away any negative energy on your big day. Perhaps even something for a good life together."

She tilted her bleach blonde head as if studying Sheri, diagnosing her energy.

And this is why she'd been unsuccessful. Apparently, the Cheramie genetics allowed for talking to the dead and praying for cures, but energy cleanses and crystal readings went too far. Raleigh knew she should be embarrassed by her closed mindedness.

Madison crossed her arms and glared at the tiny pixie. "Why don't you just do a protection spell against divorce?"

"The universe would be in disarray if we stifled its energy," Amber said, her voice flighty. "Suppose she's miserable and wants a divorce?"

Madison's right eyebrow arched, while Sheri stared at her blankly.

Better to get this over with as quickly as possible.

Motioning to the coffee table overtaken by spa supplies, Raleigh said, "You can set up. Would you like a glass of champagne?"

"No, thank you," Amber said, setting the basket down. "I don't want to blur the sight."

Sitting down on the rug, the free spirit folded her legs beneath her and began pulling candles and crystals from the basket. Stephanie and Elizabeth crowded around the table grabbing at crystals and asking about their purpose. After setting an oversized deck of tarot cards down near a silver kettle and an oversized pink crystal, Amber gazed up at Sheri.

"Did you know there's a dark energy hanging over your shoulder?" She asked, her eyes unfocused.

Sheri drew back, sinking deeper into the velvet of the chair. "What do you mean?"

Amber's fingers brushed against the surface of a jester card. "Your normally green aura has a dark black shape clinging to it."

"What does that mean?" Sheri asked, panic creeping into her voice.

Raleigh huffed. She should have answered the door and offered this doomsday harbinger a warning—possibly even a threat. The young free loader always had some dire alarm. Right now, Sheri's flight or fight reaction had been upped to death con levels. Raleigh didn't need Ms. Crystal Ball pushing her into explosive territory.

Amber shrugged, slumping forward over her crystals. "Raleigh's working on it. I can't see clearly if it will be gone in time, however. Patience should be practiced."

Sheri's face whitened and her mouth fell open. "Ummm... excuse me." She bolted from the room—clearly going check what nuclear code they'd be using next.

Raleigh sighed. She needed a vacation from this vacation.

Raleigh followed Sheri out, reaching her friend as she skidded to a stop at the kitchen sink.

"Raleigh," she panted out, her breathing haggard, "tell me what is going on?"

Grabbing her friend's shoulders, Raleigh forced Sheri to make eye contact. "I need you to breathe."

Tears brimmed her eyes, threatening to spill over. "I don't understand why any of this is happening. A week ago, we were so happy."

"I need you to take a deep breath to give that baby girl all the oxygen she needs," Raleigh said, her voice even and calm, although her insides felt queasy and jittery like a binge on coffee and Twix bars. "I need you to pay no mind to Amber. She never makes any sense."

"But, everything else," Sheri attempted to inhale, but it was jagged and curt.

"No buts," Raleigh said. "I will take care of the everything else. You are getting married tomorrow, and you will have a healthy baby girl. You can enjoy and look forward to both."

"What if we don't get married?" Sheri said. "What if I can protect the baby if I'm not selfish and I call it off."

"All nonsense," Raleigh said. "Your baby belongs to Jeff's family married or not. I will figure it out."

Madison marched in. "I have airhead hippy giving readings to Tweddle Dee and Tweddle Dum. Please don't leave me with that crew again."

Sheri laughed manically, but Raleigh frowned.

"This is all crazy," Sheri said, forcing a deep inhale and swiping at her eyes with the back of her palm.

"I know," Madison said. "We should have at least gone to the beach, so I could have a drink and bury one of them in the sand."

Raleigh only shook her head at her sister's obliviousness. It wouldn't be Madison though if she were aware of someone else's troubles.

Sheri shook herself. "Can we put some music on and remember when we were young, and life wasn't stressful?"

"Yes," Raleigh said. "Let's do that now."

Madison shrugged. "Whatever you say. This is your show."

Following her friend back into the living room, Raleigh had the frenzied feeling that she was running out of time. As if she needed to find a solution now. As if death approached—a connection drawing near.

She could not let Sheri know this, but she needed answers fast.

CHAPTER EIGHT

Hours later after chasing Amber and her odorous candles away and listening to music from their senior year of high school, Raleigh woke with a start. She listened to Sheri's deep breathing and the creaking bones of the old house cradling them inside. Getting the anxious bride to rest for her big day had been difficult. They'd escaped the slurring and mumbling of the other bridesmaids to her bedroom so Raleigh could settle Sheri down with reassurances that the wedding day tomorrow would be stress free.

From her friend's even breaths, Sheri had relaxed enough to settle into sleep.

If the house slumbered, what had wakened her?

Turning her head against her smashed pillow, she checked out the digital clock on the nightstand, a relic from when she actually needed it to wake her up and phones hadn't stolen its job permanently. 1:33.

Knowing exactly what had awakened her, she slipped out of the bed, wondering if it had disturbed the other guests spread across her house. The two bridesmaids had likely drunk too much champagne to even realize what decade they'd landed in very less where they'd curled up on the sofa. At least by morning they would believe they'd hallucinated anything they'd seen or heard. Madison would simply deny hearing anything as she preferred not to deal with any family talents these days. She'd called a hiatus.

Raleigh needn't have worried. Downstairs, no one stirred. Aunt Clarice leaned against the front doorway, wearing a short minidress in a mustard yellow color screaming seventies. Her wrinkleless complexion further backed up her chosen age for tonight's escapade. The woman enjoyed being a ghost as much as she'd liked living her single, adventurous life.

"I figured I'd wait quietly for you tonight," Aunt Clarice said, raising an arched eyebrow. "Even though we both know I like to make an entrance."

Peeking into the living room, Raleigh saw that Stephanie and Elizabeth remained stretched out on opposite ends of the sofa asleep, someone snoring. Madison occupied the spare bedroom. Her self-centered sister had insisted the two women take the living room in case they got sick from the overload of champagne. The rationale was flawed since the front bedroom was closer to the bathroom, but the two bridesmaids had been too far gone and had agreed with her.

Aunt Clarice snapped her fingers. "We best get moving. Don't want to run out of darkness before the wedding day."

"Exactly how do we go to the future?" Raleigh whispered.

All Me'Maw's warnings about knowing the future hit her at once. Visiting it felt wrong, something that could have catastrophic results.

"Glad you asked." Aunt Clarice's face lit up. "The future isn't set, so a trip there isn't as clear cut as a good cigarette and the new issue of Harper's Bazaar."

Raleigh's fear throbbed. Me'Maw always said knowledge of

the future caused a person to believe it into existence. There was danger of Raleigh doing that now.

"Don't worry, Hun," Aunt Clarice said, opening the front door. "I will show you two versions. It will be up to you to make the one you want happen."

Raleigh stood fixated to the floor. "And how do I do that?"

Aunt Clarice shrugged dramatically. "Hun, how am I supposed to know? This is the first time I take an assignment like this from those ridiculous angels that rule over us all. I would have told them to kiss my ass, but I do have a soft spot for my grandniece."

Smiling, the sassy woman motioned Raleigh forward.

Exhaling heavily, Raleigh stepped through the doorway. Darkness descended once again. Blinking against it, she opened her eyes and was standing in the living room of Sheri's house, the one that currently had a realtor sign gracing its front yard. Four weeks ago, she and Jeff had signed papers on a larger house in one of those new subdivisions not too far from Cheramie Lane. Now with the baby, Raleigh understood why they needed more space.

But this wasn't that new house that had been turned into bachelor paradise the last week.

Sheri's old, cramped living room had a Christmas tree stuffed into the corner pushed right up against that awful green recliner that her mother had proudly passed onto her. Untouched presents crowded under the tree while faux fur stockings hung from a bookshelf serving as a makeshift fireplace.

Wearing a loose black dress and clutching a box of tissues in her hand, Sheri walked in and stopped in the center of the room. Stephanie followed close behind, wearing a navy-blue pantsuit and her blonde hair pulled back tight enough to straighten the skin on her forehead.

Sheri's chest heaved heavily as she looked around the room,

her eyes sliding over Raleigh and Aunt Clarice standing in a doorway. "I want the tree down. Toss it by the road, ornaments, presents, and all. Get rid of everything."

"I'll ask your dad to help me carry it," Stephanie said, looking down at her phone screen. "He should be here any minute."

"I told him I didn't want visitors," Sheri exclaimed, choking on emotion.

Stephanie lowered her phone, tilting her head. "Everyone's just concerned. Your dad, your mom, Mike. Raleigh asked me to tell you she'd be here when you're ready to see her."

Sheri walked toward the tree. "I don't want to see her right now. She was supposed to save my girl, but instead I had to bury Corinna today."

Uneasy, Stephanie sank into the sofa corner. "She tried."

"Not hard enough," Sheri exclaimed exasperated. "Get me a garbage bag. I don't want to look at any of this anymore."

Sheri yanked the red-wrapped boxes from under the tree and tossed them onto a rug. Stephanie left the room, presumingly to go retrieve a trash bag. Scanning the room, Raleigh found a large photo of Sheri and a young girl of about five who had Sheri's eyebrows and chin with Jeff's dark hair and olive complexion. Jeff happened to be noticeably absent from the studio photograph.

Raleigh's heart broke. This future had to be changed.

With a light touch and then a grip around her wrist, Aunt Clarice squeezed, and the room disappeared into a cloud of darkness.

When the haze cleared, Raleigh stood in the living room of the new house, the one she'd recently helped move that beige sectional into place and roll out the coffee-colored rug. In the center of the room length picture window an oversized Christmas tree reached toward the ceiling with Christmas presents waving bows and shiny ribbons of at the branches as if in worship.

The thud of padded feet announced the brunette girl before she ran into the living room, sliding to her knees by the tree. She appeared to be the same age as the girl in the picture earlier, same eyebrows and olive complexion.

"Mama!" she shrilled. "Santa Clause came!"

Sheri wobbled into the room, cradling an infant against her chest. "Corrina, I told you no shouting. If you wake the baby, you won't be able to open your presents in peace."

Corinna watched her mother ease herself onto the edge of the sofa and then went over near her knees, touching the baby gently with a tiny hand. "Where's Daddy and Shawn?"

Raleigh felt the edge of blackness closing in around the corners of the room. She was running out of time, but she didn't know how this future could be possible. What had made this one happen and not the other? And how could Raleigh ensure this version?

Raleigh scoured the room for signs—anything that would help her. In the corner of the living room a toy box overflowed with dolls and stuffed animals. Stockings hung from a faux gas fireplace waiting for Papa Noel. On the mantel, garland weaved around a framed photograph of the family—Sheri, Jeff, Shawn, Corrina, and a baby. Another frame existed to the far right of Jeff and Sheri's wedding day, the two beneath a cypress tree.

The portraits documented a different life than the first version. How did Raleigh make sure this second life happened?

The scene faded into oblivion, and she and Aunt Clarice stood on the front porch of her own Acadian home.

"Our journey has ended." Aunt Clarice at least offered a look of sympathy as she spoke.

Raleigh shook her head, certain that she needed more information. "What am I supposed to do? I have no idea how to make that second life happen."

Aunt Clarice stepped further into a cloak of darkness away from the glow of the porch light. "You have the answers. As usual you just need to put the pieces together."

Raleigh said, "I'm certain I don't have enough pieces."

Aunt Clarice smiled as she began to fade. "Get some rest. Tomorrow's a big day. All will be clear in the morning."

Raleigh didn't feel as certain as Aunt Clarice. She was certain she didn't want that first future to come to pass.

That's about all she felt clear on right now.

CHAPTER NINE

Only moments later, she woke to a sense of doom nesting in her gut. Like something had gone wrong in the short time since Aunt Clarice had left her on the front porch. Sunlight streamed in through the lone window, hinting that it may be later than she'd believed. Looking over, Raleigh took in the empty expanse of her bed and her dread deepened.

Sheri had left the bed sometime between Aunt Clarice's visit and the alarm not going off.

Raleigh scrambled to get dressed, picking through the mess of clothes and shoes discarded on the floor. Wedding festivities had done a number on her house. She'd need a vacation day devoted just to cleaning up and that didn't sound any more relaxing than the last few days. Downstairs, the two champagne floozies had not stirred from the sofa, although Luna had reclaimed her favorite cushion by laying on half of Stephanie's face. Paw must have let her in through the back door this morning on his way to run his errands. Me'Maw wasn't as indulgent with her grandpup as Paw and would have not allowed the pup to continue her sleep over.

Raleigh searched the house but turned up no Sheri or note

revealing her whereabouts. As Maid of Honor, it was Raleigh's duty to have the bride at the manor for 10 A.M. for hair and makeup. At already a quarter after nine, she'd be cutting it close if she had to first locate the missing bride.

Returning to the kitchen, Raleigh discovered her cell phone buried beneath a towel and a plate filled with a half-eaten sandwich. Last night she'd made a half-hearted attempt to straighten up before giving up and herding Sheri to bed instead.

Sheri did not answer her call, which further added to that feeling of dread growing large in her belly. She tried Mike's phone next, and he answered on the third ring, his usual surfer boy morning voice muffled through the speaker.

"Did Sheri show up there this morning?" As she held the phone with her shoulder, Raleigh tried opening a bottle of aspirin with one hand. She could feel the tension beginning in her forehead. Over the last year, she'd begun to recognize this as the dead coming to visit in her head.

Fumbling and shuffling sounded from the other side the line, and Raleigh assumed Mike had drug himself out of bed to check. A breath later, he swore over the phone, his normally laid-back voice tense.

"Jeff's gone," Mike said. "He even made up the bed."

The dread in Raleigh's gut enlarged, expanding into surrounding layers.

Raleigh's mind raced over all she'd learned in three nights of Aunt Clarice's memory walks. She couldn't be certain if there was a curse or a certain mischievous Dantin spirit responsible for the tragedies.

The only fact she could hold onto from last night was Sheri had been married to Jeff in the version she'd like to be reality.

Oh no, had Sheri gone to call off the wedding? She'd mentioned it just last night.

Obviously, one version of her future had her doing just that —the version that could not happen by any means.

"We need to find them," Raleigh said, adrenaline kicking in and a tremble beginning in her fingertips. "We need to make sure this wedding happens."

A beat of silence followed as Mike processed her words, and then he said, "Married as in we don't want our two friends to ruin our group dynamic or married as in something terrible will happen if the wedding doesn't happen today?"

"Door number two."

"Oh." Mike inhaled. Raleigh imagined him running his hand through that surfer blonde hair like he always did when he began putting ideas together. "Let's get to the Manor. Everyone's scheduled to be there this morning. Someone must have seen them."

Raleigh said, "Bring Nate and Samuel. We will have a wedding today."

Mike whistled, and more rustling and moans came from the other end. "We are on our way."

Hanging up, Raleigh returned to the living room and the sleeping bridesmaids. Time to face the champagne hangovers.

A grueling twenty minutes later, she'd herded the two into her car in semi-dressed, barely presentable fashion. Raleigh felt certain when the two fully awakened she'd suffer their anger at allowing them to wear halter tops and pajama bottoms to the Dantin Manor, but Raleigh figured the bridesmaids' gowns would be what everyone saw today anyway. The two could only fault themselves for finishing off the fourth bottle of champagne last night.

In the front winding driveway of the manor, workers milled around unloading chairs and tables from a delivery truck before rolling them out toward the back gardens. Raleigh parked out of the way of the deliveries and steered the grouchy two inside, all while dialing Sheri's phone for the fourth time to no avail.

Raleigh shepherded the two inside where their footsteps echoed against the marble tiles of the foyer. Although no one walked around the airy rooms with their twelve-foot ceilings, empty vases and piles of gauzy turquoise fabric rested on rolling carts waiting for set up outside. Raleigh knew Madison had been set to arrive here before dawn, so Raleigh was surprised she hadn't made more progress. Madison had many areas that could use personal growth, but pulling a party together happened to be her area of expertise.

The three dispersed. Stephanie checked the kitchen, Elizabeth checked the ballroom, and Raleigh checked the upstairs bedroom, but all returned to the ballroom empty handed. Sheri had not escaped to Dantin Manor.

Raleigh was beginning to believe they had a runaway bride on their hands.

Out back in the gardens, Raleigh searched for Madison thinking perhaps she'd seen the bride or groom this morning. Her sister was much easier to locate as she barked insults at a young man who appeared near tears as he clutched a folding chair and stared down at his dirty tennis shoes. He couldn't be much older than twenty with his barely-there facial hair and youthful slump.

When Madison saw her sister, she dismissed the poor creature and turned on Raleigh.

"This wedding will be a disaster," Madison declared, her face flushed. "I don't know what I've done to deserve it, but someone has it out for me."

Madison tended toward the dramatic, so Raleigh surveyed the scene cautiously. Several workers were setting up rows of chairs facing what should be an arbor, but an arbor was noticeably missing. Sheri had not cared much about the wedding details. She'd allowed Madison free rein, but she'd had particular ideas about what she wanted to be married under, and it currently was lacking in the scenery. The decking around the pool where the tables were being set up for the reception was also noticeably missing the musical stage and its decorations.

A feeling of panic surged through Raleigh. "What's going on?"

"Sabotage," Madison declared emphatically. "Nothing else it can be. I *will* get to the bottom of it, but for now I need to focus on pulling this day together."

Mike approached, glancing around himself. "What's being sabotaged?"

Madison groaned. "My business?" She pulled her shoulders up and kept talking. "Since this wedding is the day after Christmas, I didn't get to do my usual check in the day before. I know it irritates vendors sometimes, but today is a perfect example of why it's necessary. Even though I do have to say the day after Christmas was just a bad choice on Sheri's part, but the bride's always right. When things didn't arrive this morning at seven o'clock like they were supposed to, I started making calls. And you know what I discovered?"

Madison gave a maniacal, high-pitched laugh. Raleigh could see the cracks in her sister's armor, which never led to good tidings.

Stephanie mumbled, hugging her bare shoulders self-consciously. "I'm guessing there was a problem."

Madison nodded. "I'd say. Someone cancelled the florist order, sent the cake to a town an hour away, fired the four-piece band, and told the caterers the wedding was at seven, not at three."

Madison stared at them a moment as if thinking through her list. Then she screeched. "This wedding is cursed!"

Jeff approached from the back doors and grimaced. "Please

don't say that too loud. I just talked Sheri into not calling off the whole thing off."

"Where is she?" Raleigh asked alarmed, glancing toward the house. Sheri didn't need any more reason to waver.

Jeff motioned toward the main house. "I delivered her upstairs. The hair and makeup people are with her now, but I assured her I'd find you and send you up."

"I'm going," Raleigh said. "We must make this wedding happen. Are we clear?"

Everyone nodded, some with confused expressions.

"Madison," Raleigh said, "I need you to pull this wedding together. What's Plan B?"

Madison huffed. "I don't know. I've never had this much go wrong before. I usually make sure this doesn't happen."

Raleigh scolded her sister. "You own this business. You took charge of your life and created this event business from scratch. You can handle a few obstacles."

Madison exhaled. "Yes, yes, I can. I can do this." She pulled her shoulders up and calmness began to return to her face. "Stephanie and Elizabeth, go to all the local florists and get flowers. I'll give you a list of what to buy."

The two nodded, although they looked caught between wanting a nap and needing Madison not to yell at them.

"Nate and Samuel, find us a band," Madison barked, picking up speed. "You two must know someone."

Nate nodded, slapping his stepbrother, Jeff, on the shoulders. The two stood at the same height although Nate's ginger hair and freckles gave away a different genetic contribution than Jeff's.

Madison continued, "I'll get on the phone with those caterers. There's no way they can't have something prepared by three."

Stephanie grumbled. "What about the cake?"

Madison straightened her shoulders. "Two hours out of the way can still make it here. I don't care if they are setting up while Sheri is walking down the aisle."

Her sister's cracks were showing a little less. On a day like today, Raleigh could offer no complaints about her sister's steel edges.

Raleigh said, "Mike and Jeff, find some volunteers to set up that arbor. Sheri had her heart set on that tree branch monstrosity."

The two nodded, both wore determined expressions as they glanced toward the unassembled pile of limbs.

"And what are you going to do?" Stephanie asked, a hint of that jealousy she'd been harboring slipping in even though she looked ready to keel over.

Raleigh grimaced. "Talk to the ghosts of two little girls and kindly ask that they stop interfering."

Jeff rubbed his hand over this morning's stubble. "Do you think that will work?"

Raleigh shrugged. "I'm not certain they caused any of this. This feels awfully human. But from what I've been shown, if you two get married, everything will be alright."

Jeff's eyes widened as Raleigh's news sank in. Then, his forehead wrinkled in determination. "Let's make this wedding happen. And let's not mention anything to Sheri. I'd like her to remember our wedding day as somewhat of a good day."

Madison clapped her hands together, already beginning to walk toward the workers setting up tables. "Hurry people. Time is short. Raleigh, next time get rid of the ghosts before we plan a wedding. Geez, those girls are lucky I'm not the one dealing with them."

Raleigh moved to hurry toward her task, but Mike clasped her hand, squeezed, and pulled her in, breathing her scent in deep.

"Save me a dance, Spirit Walker," he whispered, "That's how certain I am that you can handle those two."

Raleigh leaned into him, inhaling sandalwood and a hint of beach balm. She allowed another moment to feel his confidence flow through her, and then she left to go inside to wrangle the wedding crashers.

She'd only made it to the front stairs when Alcee Dantin strolled in through the front door carrying tuxedo garment bags slung over his shoulder.

"Big day today," he said, nodding in Raleigh's direction, looking at her forehead instead of her eyes.

Raleigh hesitated to take the first step up the riser. She hadn't had the opportunity to speak to Horace or Alcee about their sister. Either may be able to clear up some of Raleigh's indecision about what to do with the menace.

"Do you mind if I ask about your family?" Raleigh said, watching the change of his expression, she figured he did mind.

"I don't really see much of them," Alcee said, shifting the hangers to his arm. "You probably want to ask my mother or brother."

Raleigh shook her head, looking him in the eyes. "No, I have a rather strange question for you, but I'm sure you have heard things about me before, so the weirdness shouldn't be completely unexpected."

Alcee stared at her a moment, and she held her breath that he wouldn't pretend his sons—or the entire town—had not been talking for the last year about her conversing with the dead.

Finally, he offered her a curt nod.

"When you saw Claudette's ghost the day your daughter died," Raleigh gulped, trying to get it all out as Alcee visibly paled, "did you freeze from surprise, fear, shock, what? Did you not understand what she wanted?"

Alcee's body seemed to slump into the garment bags as he

closed his eyes. She regretted bringing it up as she watched him relive his pain.

He swallowed, looking down at his scuffed tennis shoes. "I was shocked. I'd never seen her before. Horace had confessed that he'd seen Claudette once when he'd been distraught, but I figured it was his subconscious. Lord knows he has plenty of reasons to feel guilty. But she was so clearly there. I couldn't even focus on her words, just the image of her looking exactly as she had when we were kids."

"And then you realized the kids were in the pool?" Raleigh prompted, dragging him out of whatever his mind had fixated on just now that caused his entire body to crumple.

Alcee nodded. "I saw Jeff and I thought she'd warned me about him. But... but..." Alcee trailed off. "I suppose you know the rest?"

Raleigh leaned against the banister. "The common theory right now is that the ghost of Claudette is attempting to ruin the wedding." She figured she'd spare him some of the painful details. "I'm not certain it's her though."

Alcee grimaced. "I've stayed away from this place for years, and Claudette's ghost has not been what has kept me away."

Raleigh peered at him closely. He looked like he wanted to say something but hesitated to share anything personal with her. "Someone I should be worried about as I try to save the wedding?"

Alcee shrugged. "I'm trying to let bygones be bygones since my mother offered to play host for the wedding."

"Eliza seems to love Jeff and Sheri together."

Alcee nodded. "My mother tends to be kept in the dark when things are wrong."

"What about Horace then?" Raleigh asked. "How guilty is his conscious?"

Alcee sighed. "True, I'm not my brother's biggest fan, but he's not much of a doer. More like an opportunist."

"What do you mean?"

"I can't tell you what he's been up to recently," Alcee said, looking around the hideous foyer. "But I can tell you what he did back then."

Raleigh exhaled, figuring she may be able to get somewhere with more information.

"About six months after my daughter's funeral, I caught Horace and my wife together in his bedroom." Alcee gritted his teeth. "Margot swore that it hadn't been going on for long, but the two had bonded over a secret, one they didn't want me to find out."

Raleigh listened, feeling as she always did when she found out family secrets she shouldn't know—ghosts were so much less complicated than the people they'd left behind.

A look of pure anger flared Alcee's nostrils. "Uncle Mathis had molested my daughter for months before she'd died," Alcee spit out. "Both of them had known and not said anything for selfish reasons. My wife, because she didn't want to risk not inheriting Dantin manor if things didn't go right in a confrontation, and Horace because my uncle had been paying him off."

Raleigh felt as though the floor would open and swallow her. She felt completely disgusted with these people right now.

"Your wife didn't run away with a guitar player." Raleigh stated simply.

"Oh, she ran away," Alcee said. "She left in shame when I wouldn't forgive her, more for our daughter than the cheating. She ended up with a guitar player, and then a bartender, and then an accountant."

Raleigh thought about the room upstairs with the beds, all waiting on the girls. "What about Eliza? Did she know?"

Alcee shook his head. "I didn't have the heart to tell her.

Besides, I have a feeling that Uncle Mathis wasn't just disinherited by my grandfather. Jo Ellen has a theory that he did this to Eliza when she was younger and that's why he was disinherited. I mean, the story my mother believes is not realistic for that era when laws would have said differently of a daughter inheriting over a son. Uncle Mathis has about ten years over my mother, so it would be about right for her to be too young to remember when he was chased off."

Raleigh shuddered. The human element had taken a dark turn.

But as far as Raleigh knew the uncle had not been around for any of the wedding festivities yet. He couldn't have even had access to the wedding information.

Alcee exhaled, looking around the room. "It's funny how all these years I've focused so much on the bad memories of this place, I've forgotten that there were any good."

Raleigh nodded. "We tend to do that as humans... and as spirits."

Because Raleigh had just had a thought. Claudette had even more reason to haunt this family and cause it misery. In a twisted way, she may believe she was protecting the girls. Since if Eliza had suffered and Rebecca had suffered, Raleigh would be willing to bet that Claudette had also suffered at the hands of Uncle Mathis.

CHAPTER TEN

At the top of the stairs, Raleigh heard soothing voices from Sheri's ajar bedroom door—one male and one female. From the animated conversations, they seemed acquainted with each other. As fellow stylists, they'd likely attended conventions or trainings together. Even in a small town, Sheri liked to stay up to date.

In a bid to keep the whole wedding low-key, Sheri had wanted to do her own hair and make-up, but Eliza had insisted on some level of pampering fit for a bride. The family matriarch had won out based on the argument that all brides deserved to be the center of attention for this one day since marriage itself forced them to compromise for the remainder of their lives.

Raleigh didn't want to weigh in on that topic, but with Eliza's pampering insistence, the outspoken woman had inadvertently bought Raleigh a few more minutes to speak to the mischievous spirits inhabiting the lavender room.

Slipping into the bedroom, she caught Claudette brushing her hair before the vanity with a silver-plated brush. The thin girl wore a silk empire waist gown in an ecru color, one of the accent colors of Sheri's wedding.

"Preparing for the wedding?" Raleigh asked, seeing her reflection in the mirror. She needed to tone her facial sarcasm down.

Claudette smirked. "If it happens."

Entering the room, Raleigh sank onto the corner of the first bed. "Are you against this wedding for some reason?"

Claudette brushed her brown curls, which sprung up as she reached the end with that tarnished silver brush. She didn't look at Raleigh as she responded. "Weddings and parties don't really matter to me."

"What if this wedding led to a Dantin girl coming to live in the Manor?" Raleigh studied her expression, waiting for a sign to reveal the girl's intention.

Claudette paused in her brushing, clutching the object tightly to her chest. "No Dantin girls."

Raleigh lowered her voice as if conspiring with her. "Do you know why all the Dantin girls end up like you?"

Claudette frowned. "No one can save them."

"And you have tried?"

Glaring at Raleigh, she returned to brushing her hair. "Girls will never live here, and I will never have to share my mother."

Raleigh inhaled loudly, slumping back into the frilly lilac bedspread. For just a moment, she'd begun to believe that Claudette hadn't been responsible for the chaos. Then, the vengeful girl said something like this, and Raleigh's confidence in her conclusion wavered.

Rebecca shimmered in near the closet, wearing the same dress as Claudette. Clearly the two fancied themselves wedding guests, possibly even wedding party members. Rebecca peered at Raleigh curiously before looking over at Claudette.

"I've come to ask for help with your brother's wedding." Raleigh directed this at Rebecca, hoping to appeal to her love for her sibling. "I'd like to ensure it happen without any issue."

"My brother?" Rebecca asked, her forehead crinkled in thought.

"Yes, Jeff. Your brother remembers you visiting him when he was young," Raleigh said. "He's missed having his sister around."

Rebecca's face crumpled.

"Don't listen to her," Claudette said, turning on the vanity stool. "She only wants to save another Dantin girl. She's probably lying."

"And why would saving a Dantin girl be bad?" Raleigh asked. "Your mama is getting old. She won't live forever, and someone will need to take care of this house. Without a girl to inherit, it will be Horace."

Claudette glowered at Raleigh, handing the brush over to Rebecca. "What if no one gets the Manor?"

Raleigh said, "Then it will be sold to a stranger who will empty your room of all your furniture and belongings."

Claudette huffed, turning back toward the mirror.

"Jeff remembers me?" Rebecca asked, her voice uncertain.

Raleigh smiled, aching at the faded, not fully formed girl before her. The child at the pool had possessed so much determination and heart, but the one before her remained only a shadow. "He mostly remembers you as a playmate. But, yes, he knows it was you."

Standing still, Rebecca gripped the brush tightly in her hands and hung onto Raleigh's words.

"Well girls," Raleigh said, standing. "My job is to make sure this wedding happens. Do you think you could help me with that?"

Rebecca nodded, but Claudette's reflection glared at Raleigh in the mirror, anger darkening her angelic face.

Raleigh raised an eyebrow in response. "What if you agree

to not cancel caterers or wedding cakes or all the wedding things?"

Claudette pursed her lips. "Not my style."

Raleigh nodded, trying to judge from her haughty expression if she were telling the truth. "Perhaps you should consider what would make your mother happy. She'd really like to pass this house down to a girl and not to Horace."

Claudette's reflection continued to glower at her as she smoothed out wrinkles in the fabric of her dress.

Raleigh couldn't tell what impact she'd made at all and decided she might have better luck with Sheri.

In the disheveled room across the hall, Clint Ryan fussed over Sheri's pin-up curls while Phoebe Astonia stood by waiting to add the next layer to her face. Clutching a tissue in her fist, Sheri appeared ready to bolt as her jittery nerves rocked her back and forth.

Sheri's green eyes found Raleigh's as she stepped inside the room and closed the door. "Finally!"

Raleigh smiled, trying not to think about the conversations she'd had on the way up to this room. She didn't want them showing in her face. The confidence in her plan had grown shaky—what little plan she had of getting the two hitched today and it all working itself out.

Sheri stood, pushing Clint's hand away from her hair. "Please give me a moment with my maid of honor. Why don't you two go to the kitchen and check on those mimosas? I'm sure the other bridesmaids will be here soon, and you can get started on them."

Behind Sheri's half-finished hair, Clint and Phoebe exchanged looks, but they each put down their tools and retreated from the room.

Sheri waited for the door to click closed behind the two well-groomed stylists and then she padded over to Raleigh. "I'm going to ask you for a favor, and as Maid of Honor, you can't refuse."

Raleigh gazed up at her friend in response. Sheri rose about three inches over her own 5'6" height. The woman had reached this height in sixth grade, and massive teasing had resulted from boys who came to her hips.

Sheri swallowed. "I know it sounds crazy, but I need you to get me out of here. I can't go through with this wedding."

"Explain." Raleigh crossed her arms across her chest, her brain beginning to fire with plans to get the woman down the aisle. Raleigh was not above knocking her out with some over the counter sleep meds. The idea sounded bad even as she had it.

"I have this panic in my throat," Sheri said, clasping at her neck. "It's running through my body like ants crawling on me. I can't risk the baby. That's insane to me, and yes, I know I sound crazy."

"Sit down," Raleigh said, leading her toward the bed.

"We should be trying to sneak out of here," Sheri said, turning back toward the door. "I've heard the whispers about how my wedding is a disaster. How is this my dream day?"

Raleigh exhaled. People talked too loud and too much. "The wedding plans are being handled as we speak."

"Don't you think it's a sign?" Sheri exclaimed. "I mean when your wedding falls apart, you should probably listen."

Shaking her head, Raleigh pulled her down next to her on the edge of the bed. "Last night I saw two versions of your future. One where you had two babies and one where you had none. You know what the only difference between those two lives were?"

"My sanity?" Sheri groaned, slumping forward.

"No," Raleigh said, squeezing her hand. "You and Jeff were married."

Sheri's haggard breaths filled the room as Raleigh's words sank through her panic.

"So, everything will turn out okay if I walk down the aisle today, even if the wedding is such a mess no one shows up to marry us?" Sheri dabbed at her eye with a tissue, her voice cracking.

"The ceremony details are being worked out. You will be married today, even if you end up with just that simple back-yard wedding you originally wanted."

"I'm getting married." Sheri laughed, the sound gathering from her chest and growing louder and deeper.

She glanced over at Raleigh, both eyebrows fully arched. "*Married.*"

"I know," Raleigh said. "That poufy dress that looks like a wedding cake hanging in that closet proves it."

Sheri shook her head. "I've been so focused on worrying about what could go wrong, I haven't let myself believe it would actually happen. But it is, huh?"

"It is, so let's get you ready," Raleigh said. "The photographer will be here shortly, and none of us want to preserve the before the glitz and glam look."

"Who cares?" Sheri said, laughing manically again. "All I need is the groom and an officiant."

Raleigh laughed in relief, hoping Madison had checked on Father Lucas. Perhaps she should give the local priest a call.

A soft rapt came on the door right before it opened, and Eliza wobbled in wearing a festive cranberry pantsuit. Raleigh suspected this to be a pre-wedding outfit as the woman seemed to love a good wardrobe change as much as Aunt Clarice.

"I just wanted to slip in before all the bustle began and bring you this," Eliza lumbered over and handed over a small black velvet bag.

Sheri accepted the item, looking at it as if it would prick her and she'd fall under a sleeping curse.

"I know you aren't much on wedding traditions," Eliza said with a slight smile, "but I thought you might like something borrowed and blue."

Sheri slipped a small pearl bracelet out with a center sapphire stone set in an intricate silver filigree pattern. Raleigh had never seen something so delicate or beautiful.

Sheri looked up, her eyes misting. Eliza clasped her hand around Sheri's holding the bracelet.

"My mother gave this to me as an engagement gift," Eliza's eyes watered. "She had unique but modest taste, and I loved it dearly. I thought my own daughter would inherit it and wear it on her wedding day..." Eliza inhaled deeply. "But that was not to be. My daughters-in-law each claimed it didn't fit their style, but you have just enough personality to carry it."

Sheri nodded, allowing Eliza to slip it on her wrist.

To give them a moment, Raleigh stepped back as the two embraced and saw Claudette standing in the door frame, glaring at the two.

Panic began to flood through Raleigh. This would not likely go over well with this messy spirit.

CHAPTER ELEVEN

The chords of the wedding march strummed a third refrain, and concern rustled through the crowd. Maintaining her picture-ready smile, Raleigh peered around the standing crowd searching for any sign of the stalled bride's appearance at the foot of the aisle. Only moments before, she'd left Sheri in the aviary all set to begin, even with the last-minute change of itinerary. Originally, Madison's agenda had called for the promenade from a secluded area of the side gardens, but the guests had refused to be corralled into their seats even with Madison's curt directives. Oblivious, this crowd preferred to mingle at an outdoor wedding instead of sitting in the pretty draped chairs.

On a beat longer than comfortable, Sheri appeared at the back of the aisle. Although her cheeks appeared a darker pink than a moment ago, her smile held as she looked ahead toward the group at the altar, her eyes searching for Jeff. The two smiled at each other—a genuine smile, and Raleigh thought this is why people cried at weddings.

Standing at Sheri's side, her son Shawn's smile faltered, and his attention darted to all the people staring at them from their seats. From her position to the left of the arbor, Raleigh could see the boy's trembling body. Sheri had elected for her son to walk her down the aisle after her father had shown up hammered an hour ago. Having expected it, Sheri had prepared Shawn as a backup plan, but the ten-year-old seemed to regret agreeing to it now. Raleigh wondered if his nerves would hold up under the entire trek to the front.

Raleigh glanced over at Mike, and he smiled, his eyes already on her. The two had not discussed weddings or anything permanent—though that didn't mean it wasn't under consideration. Raleigh figured she should proceed cautiously with one failed engagement and another recent failed relationship. But still, weddings had a way of making a girl dream about her own. She'd snap out of it tomorrow.

Reaching the front altar, Sheri beamed at Jeff. As Raleigh moved in to collect her Calli lily bouquet, Sheri mumbled through her big smile. "Someone locked me inside."

Raleigh exhaled, wondering if a certain mischievous spirit had attempted one last ditch effort to stop the wedding. Claudette hadn't looked pleased about the bracelet, but the afternoon had been uneventful, and the ceremony details had fallen into place. Raleigh had mistakenly believed that she'd made an impact with her talk.

Of course, the culprit could be someone of the human variety—not a spirit at all.

Raleigh scanned the attendees gathered in the rows of white folding chairs. Several individuals had come in after she'd walked down the aisle by Mike's side. Jeff's flower girl niece and ring bearer nephew had run down the aisle behind the two. The laugh of the audience had distracted from the last-minute stragglers filling in the empty seats. Teenagers had shuffled into the last two rows on the groom's side, all adolescents Raleigh hadn't seen before. Eliza's brother had been escorted to a front row by Horace, with his rather sleek, carved cane leading the way. An uncle or two of Sheri's in shiny maroon polyester suits had lumbered to a back chair buckling their suit jackets as they walked.

Anyone of these late comers could have walked near the aviary and locked Sheri inside to delay the wedding. Of course, the easier answer involved two young spirits intervening again.

Raleigh wasn't convinced of their guilt though. Claudette's motives weren't clear. Why would she have wanted to save the last two Dantin girls yet prevent a wedding from happening?

Father Lucas began the ceremony while Raleigh looked out at the crowd, searching for any strange happenings in the audience that would indicate interference. Eliza beamed at the couple, while Sheri's father slumped in his chair with his eyes half closed.

On the second row, Sheri's aunt and uncle were bickering, their voices growing louder, attracting attention from the guests around them. Raleigh was so engrossed by the back and forth between the two that the sudden appearance of Claudette before her rocked her back on the uncomfortable strappy silver heels she wore.

"Save her," Claudette said, her eyes fiery and haunting.

Hearing a cracking sound, Raleigh lunged toward Sheri without thinking.

At the same moment as Raleigh moved in, Jeff glanced up. The elaborate tree branches woven into an arched arbor cracked and collapsed.

Jeff pulled Sheri toward him, and Raleigh yanked Father Lucas by the loose fabric of his black shirt, feeling certain that she'd probably earn penance in hell for touching a man of God. She couldn't quite work out the details in her head with the serotonin and cortisol increase pumping through her veins.

The arbor crashed to kindle on the makeshift floor, scraping against Raleigh's leg as she moved out of the way.

As Jeff clung tightly to Sheri, the bride appeared caught between tears and laughter. Raleigh made sure Father Lucas stood upright before checking on Sheri.

Sheri gulped. "Are you sure this isn't a sign, Raleigh? Tell me this isn't a sign that I'm supposed to run."

Raleigh squeezed the woman's trembling hand. "This is only a sign that someone is trying to destroy your happiness, and we aren't going to allow it."

Mike grimaced over the remnants of the twigs, and Raleigh shifted her body to block it from Sheri's view.

Raleigh clearly should have monitored the construction of the arbor or at least assigned it to someone competent. She wondered if Mike and Jeff had done it themselves or enlisted help. Since both worked in construction, she'd hazard to guess, someone else had worked on it. Otherwise, this would not have been another mishap for this wedding.

Surveying the damage, Father Lucas seemed unfazed by the near-death experience as he looked out at the concerned, gaping guests. Taking a few steps toward Sheri, he smiled as he gathered her hands in his. "Shall we continue?"

Sheri laughed, near hysterics. "Yes, let's say the I dos before something else happens."

Father Lucas chuckled, patting her gently. "Let's say a prayer that the excitement brings the two of you a blessed, happy marriage."

Looking murderous, Madison orchestrated everyone back into place, staging them in front of the disaster area to block it from the view of the audience and the photographer. Within five minutes, Father Lucas had the two married.

Raleigh exhaled, the relief making her muscles feel like mush. The two were married. Crisis diverted.

With the strum of the wedding march, Raleigh joined Mike for their trek back up the aisle toward the poolside reception.

Mike leaned in and whispered. "The arbor was cut. It didn't fall on its own."

Raleigh felt the tension flush back through her. "And I doubt two little spirits did the cutting." The two stopped and smiled for the photographer as thoughts raced through her head.

The arbor had to be a person, not misguided Claudette. A human saboteur felt more devious somehow. Not to mention, something that wouldn't end with a wedding. She'd been wrong about it ending with them getting married. She could see that now. That didn't mean it didn't end at this wedding. She needed to discover who had tried to prevent this wedding from happening and why. She had a three-hour reception to pull it together.

CHAPTER TWELVE

Handing Sheri's Uncle Phillip a pin, Raleigh pointed him toward the back of the growing dance line and scanned the lively crowd all while keeping a protective eye on Sheri. After the father-daughter dance debacle, Monty, the lead singer in the band, had quickly called for the money dance and the crowd had responded to the Southern Louisiana tradition of pinning money on the bride to dance with her.

Sheri's father had drug himself to the dance floor, attempted to take the microphone for a speech that had been too slurred to understand, and then tripped over one of the lanterns surrounding the dance floor. He'd spewed blood on the white roses nearby, and Madison had quickly ushered him off. Sheri would have preferred to go hide a moment in her humiliation as everyone whispered, but Monty had called her and Jeff to the dance floor.

"This is humiliating," Sheri said, smiling at those who approached. "We are begging for money at the manor of millionaires who are now my in-laws."

Raleigh laughed. "But you aren't worth millions, my friend. You are a hair stylist and Jeff's in construction. Just consider the money as a silver lining to this day. I hear diapers are expensive."

"It's embarrassing," Sheri said, smoothing out the chiffon layer of her dress. "Only a Cajun would hatch a tradition around pinning money to an expensive wedding dress."

Handing a pin to Sheri's mother, Raleigh continued smiling as the band wound down a rowdy country music tune. Nate and Samuel had rounded up the regular band from the local bar that Raleigh, Mike, and Sheri frequented. The drummer had played basketball with Jeff in high school and had been happy to play a few hours, especially since they'd been off until New Year's Eve.

"No pinning on that beautiful dress. Tuck it in this satin bag," Raleigh said, slipping the delicate satin straps onto Sheri's wrist. "You will manage just like every poor Cajun girl before you. And you know why?"

"Why?" Sheri grumbled.

"Because you are married, and your little one is safe." Raleigh raised an eyebrow and smiled.

Sheri laughed before sashaying onto the dance floor at the opening strums of "New Orleans Lady." The line cheered and Sheri welcomed one of the distant Dantin cousins as her first spin.

Raleigh distributed pins as she watched the crowd. Even with her assurance to Sheri, she wasn't certain Sheri and the baby were safe. Certainly, something sinister must be going on, but the crowd mingled, nibbling on mini crawfish pies and fried fish and boudin balls as waiters walked around with trays. Most of Jeff's relatives she couldn't put a name to, and Sheri's family had camped out near the bar and were heartily enjoying the free mixed drinks. Cousin Joey and his wife had helped Me'Maw and Paw to a table and the two swayed to the music enjoying the conversation as people stopped by their table to say hello. No one appeared ready to cause any more disasters besides the already destroyed arbor.

As the dance line began to lessen and Raleigh could get a more thorough view of the wedding area, she spotted Claudette on the sidelines near an arrangement of white rose stems. Handing the pins off to Stephanie who'd stood nearby salivating over the task, Raleigh walked toward the girl, conscious of how it would look to the guests. Although most of Barbeaux Bayou knew she was traiteur to the dead, they didn't want to witness her perform anything associated with such a title. Tolerance only extended so far in small towns.

The vengeful child glared at her as she approached, but she didn't flicker out. At least that was a start.

"Are you enjoying the wedding?" Raleigh asked, straightening the vase on the column.

Claudette huffed, crossing her arms across her chest. "It's not a complete disaster."

Contemplating Claudette's bitterness, Raleigh watched Sheri finish a dance with Nate before twirling into Samuel's outstretched arms. Maybe she'd instilled too much faith in the girl. Perhaps she had been responsible for everything over the last few days. Raleigh had seen enough to know that anything was possible.

"Thank you for warning me earlier," Raleigh said, trying again.

"I suppose one Dantin man may not be terrible," Claudette said. "Time will tell."

"Are they really all terrible or perhaps maybe you frightened them?" Raleigh asked. "Most people tend to be afraid of a ghost."

Claudette pouted and glared at Raleigh. "Terrible. Uncle Mathis and Horace did horrible things."

"Maybe you helped change that tonight."

Claudette glared at her. "I'm still dead and those men are alive."

"Did you tell anyone about your Uncle Mathis?" Raleigh asked.

Claudette's face darkened. "I told Horace. He was supposed to help me, but then he dropped me. I know he did it on purpose. I saw it in his eyes."

"What about Alcee? Your mother?"

Claudette shook her head. "Uncle Mathis told me he'd hurt Mama. Horace said he'd help me tell father. But he didn't. The Dantin men are terrible. They hide secrets and all the girls die."

The vengeful seven-year-old faded into the plaster column holding an antique pewter vase.

Although Raleigh couldn't argue with Claudette's logic, she also didn't feel as though she was reaching the stubborn spirit. Forgiveness didn't seem in her nature, and Raleigh didn't know what sort of justice she could achieve at this point. She'd actually need to have some evidence of something to even prove it wasn't the vengeful little girl instead of a human culprit. She may have to call in Aunt Clarice to reach the girl, and her glamorous aunt didn't have a soft spot for children.

Madison strolled over, carrying a cake knife and a silver tray. "You're talking to yourself again. You should really get that checked out."

Raleigh ignored her. The two were at an impasse right now with Madison's training. Her sister had been chosen to be the next traiteur, Me'Maw's replacement one day, but she'd decided she'd prefer not to do so. "You managed to pull the wedding off," Raleigh commented instead.

"Don't jinx me," Madison said, surveying the crowd, "It's not over yet."

Leaving a group of men gathered on the sidelines by the

dance floor, Mike walked in her direction, waving at a few people waiting for their turn in the dance line.

Approaching, he glanced around before he said, "So who do you think tried to ruin the wedding?"

Raleigh smiled up at him as he pulled her close, his tux hugging all the right places.

"Didn't you and Jeff take care of that beautiful, deadly arbor?"

Mike grinned, running a thumb along her shoulder. "We didn't cut the branches, but I'm sure the florist will make them pay for the damage."

"Yes, yes, add it to the growing list," Madison said, placing the platter down on a side table. "Why is my son talking to himself? Did he catch what you have?"

Scanning the crowd, Raleigh found Mason sitting at a table near the edge of an outside group of tables. His hands moved and his face contorted and contracted in excitement as he spoke to Rebecca who sat in the chair next to him. The two conversed as if they were sitting at a lunch table at school without a care in the world.

Gaping at them for a moment, Raleigh watched the conversation as if they were a vaudeville show.

Alarmed, Madison looked away from Raleigh and back toward Mason. "What is it?"

"You won't like this," Raleigh whispered.

"Get on with it, Raleigh," Madison exclaimed. "You're scaring me."

"He's talking to Jeff's sister, Rebecca."

"What sister? Jeff doesn't have a sister." Madison said, her eyes searching the table. "You mean the one that's dead?"

Madison's pitch rose and panic crept in.

Continuing to watch the conversation, Raleigh nodded. She couldn't pinpoint the exact age she'd discovered her abilities—

she'd been young when children had started to reach her as they'd died. She'd been confused, and Me'Maw had helped her. Her Paw's voice had calmed her through the experiences. She hadn't dealt with ghosts though until she'd moved into the house with Aunt Clarice and inherited a house guest.

A hard thwack came down on her arm. "Well, don't just stand there. Do something!" Madison exclaimed. "Make it stop."

Raleigh rubbed her arm against the stinging. "Relax. It could be nothing. Children supposedly see ghosts more than adults."

Raleigh did not believe that in this case. With the Cheramie genetics, Raleigh was certain that Mason had become the next generation of her. She most certainly would not have that discussion at Sheri's wedding as Madison would ruin the whole day with a rant about their genetic curse.

"Still," Madison said, her body remaining tense. "People will think he's strange. Go talk to him."

Mike twisted his lip. "Most will believe he has an imaginary friend. He's old enough for that."

A contemplative look washed over Madison, and she bit down on her lips, studying her son.

"I'm going," Raleigh said. Mike squeezed her hand and released her from his grip. He hadn't made his peace yet with the ghosts—only the theory of them.

As Raleigh approached the table, Rebecca shimmered away.

Raleigh pulled out a chair and slid in next to Mason. "Did you make a new friend?"

Mason scolded her with his cute, chubby cheek face. "Nanan, she's a see-through girl."

"Yes, I can see that," Raleigh said, studying her nephew's long eyelashes and dark brown hair flipping onto his forehead. "I wasn't aware that you could see the see-through people."

Mason stuck a fork in a meatball. "I'm a smart six-year-old."

"Yes, you are," Raleigh said. "Have you seen any other see-through friends?"

Mason shrugged. "There's a girl in the neighborhood. She comes play sometimes. She's not as nice as Rebecca though."

"And you never mentioned these visits to your mama, I suppose," Raleigh said.

Mason stuck the entire meatball in his mouth and shook his head.

"That's probably a good idea," Raleigh said. "I'd probably also not mention it to your dad either."

Mason grinned, barbecue sauce staining his white teeth.

Mason's father had a particular dislike for Raleigh since high school—Raleigh had turned his repeated advances down back then. Any similarities between Raleigh and his son would be drilled out of the impressionable boy. Jeffrey Zedeaux's only saving grace was that he had a sweet spot for Madison and loved his son. Raleigh remained quiet on the man for these two reasons alone.

"Did Rebecca have anything interesting to say about the wedding?" Raleigh asked.

Mason shrugged. "She did have a message for you."

His forehead and lips scrunched together in concentration. Mason's memory did not allow for more than a few seconds at a time most days—especially when it came to chores.

"Do you remember what it was about?" Raleigh prompted.

"A man in the library," Mason said. "I can't remember all what she said. She talked so much, Nanan."

"Do you remember anything about this man in the library?"

Mason stabbed another meatball. "A deal? Something going on in the library. A bad man. Ohh... I remember she said something about a thief. Stealing a house."

On reflex, Raleigh looked toward the manor and then

scanned the wedding guests mingling around the outside tables. Cousin Joey had just handed Me'Maw and Paw cups, and she could see him scanning the crowd. He'd become jumpy recently after all the detective work he'd been doing.

"Nanan," Mason said, "how do you steal a house?"

Raleigh muttered, "Carefully." Considering everything she had learned about this family and the certain key people missing from the wedding currently, she knew what was happening.

The wedding may have brought safety to Sheri's baby, but unknowingly they'd put someone else in danger.

CHAPTER THIRTEEN

Raleigh had never made so many phone calls and pushed as many people's buttons as she had in the last fifteen minutes. All while managing to keep the impending trouble from reaching the mingling bride. This last bit had taken a little finesse—a skill she failed at miserably on a daily basis.

Bracing herself, she pushed the library door open of Dantin Manor, a room she hadn't had any real occasion to step inside during her visits this week. With deep mahogany paneling typical of an earlier time and rows of leather spines embossed in small letters to reveal dusty titles, the room felt like a somber tomb. To complete the look, a large monstrosity of a desk sat in the middle of the room. Currently, two gentlemen sat facing each other in leather wing back chairs studying documents on the deep cherry surface.

Horace looked up immediately as she entered. "What are you doing? Isn't this an outside wedding?"

Raleigh smiled, continuing to walk into the center of the room. Claudette appeared in the corner by a standing globe, watching her carefully. "I thought I'd join this party. Figured your mother and I's invitation were lost in all the chaos the last few days."

Eliza wobbled in, her cane leading the way. The navy-blue beaded pant suit gave off a regal air. "I've been informed that you two scoundrels have been up to no good."

Her eyes lay upon them harshly and Claudette's attention turned toward her mother.

"Now Eliza," Mathis said twisting in his seat. "Family should always refrain from harsh judgements about each other, don't you think?"

Raleigh stood, towering over their seated positions, placing herself in viewing of the documents spread out on the surface of the desk.

"Sabotaging a family's wedding doesn't inspire loyalty."

"You can't prove any of that. You are reaching," Horace said as he covered the documents with an oversized book that lay haphazardly on the edge.

"Actually, we can." Raleigh watched as Cousin Joey strolled into the room, appearing official in his sheriff's office jacket. The navy-blue overcoat had been in the backseat of his truck and seriously clashed with his dress shirt and slacks, but he believed in always being professional.

"You brought the Barbeaux police to a wedding?" Mathis said, disgust curling his bottom lip. "Your family line has grown diluted and weak. You should cut your losses, Eliza."

"We didn't sabotage the wedding," Horace repeated, staring at Uncle Joey, his eyes never rising above the jacket.

Joey whipped out a paper from inside the pocket of his coat. "The cancellation calls came from the private line of this office. Raleigh asked me this morning to trace those calls, and we weren't certain who'd made them. But I have two eyewitnesses that will place you at the arbor."

Mathis shook his head and strummed his fingers on the arm

of the chair. "Such a scoundrel. Sissy, you didn't do a good job raising this one. My sons don't behave this way."

Horace's face reddened, his anger choking him. Reaching over, Raleigh snatched the documents under the book, crinkling them in the process.

"All of that may be true, Mathis," Raleigh said, scanning the signature lines of the document, "except you are the one trying to steal the Manor."

"Absurd," Mathis uttered, wrinkling his nose. "I can't steal my family home which belongs to me just as much as any of my siblings."

"It doesn't belong to you anymore," Eliza said, bracing both hands on her cane. "Father left it to me and Alfredo."

Mathis stood, smiling down at his sister. Claudette eased back into the wall of books.

"Perhaps, but you decided to write some ridiculous inheritance clause that willed it to the first-born girl or to a son with a family. Your family members do not qualify. In such an instance, all remaining Dantin's have a claim. Father's will specifically stated if you had no heir, the manor went to a sibling so that it could remain in the family."

"Except you both knew that was going to change, which is why you are transferring the deed now," Raleigh said.

Mathis glared at her. "I'm sure I don't have any idea what you are speaking about."

Raleigh handed the documents over to Joey. "Horace over-heard Sheri and I speaking the day of the engagement party. I heard the door, but I didn't realize Horace was spying. Sheri is pregnant with a girl, and Eliza will have her heir."

Eliza's cane came down on the floor. "And you tried to make sure it didn't happen?"

Horace shook his head. "Mother, this is character assignation. I would never do anything to hurt this family. She can't prove I'm involved in any of this."

Eliza looked down at her son with a distaste she seemed to reserve only for him. Raleigh would feel sorry for him if he hadn't been so manipulative and nearly cost Sheri her wedding or life with the arbor incident.

Horace appealed to the others. "Mathis wanted the house, so he had his lawyer draw up papers. He promised that if I helped him, I could stay here and mange it. Uncle Mathis is responsible."

Mathis glared down at him, his lips twitching. "A difficult theory for you to prove nephew. And with a female inheriting, the only one set to benefit would be you. Everything points to you, not me."

"That's completely unfair," Horace stuttered out. "I would not have put my mother in a home. That was your intentions."

A small gasp escaped involuntarily from Eliza and her body tensed.

"And what were the plans for the Manors other residents?" Raleigh asked, drawing their attention from Eliza's growing anger.

"Other res..." Horace trailed off. "No one lives here but me and mother."

"The three girls of your family haven't left this home," Raleigh said. "As far as I can gather, they don't really like either of you. I can't imagine what they'd do if you remove Eliza."

Horace's face blanched. "I don't believe in ghosts."

"Really? Because Claudette's standing only feet from you," Raleigh said. "She believes you pulled her down that tree. What do you think?"

Eliza gasped, her spotted hand trembled as she covered her mouth.

"You're crazy," Horace said, his eyes growing wide.

"She will haunt you until you tell the truth," Raleigh said. "Do you feel her near your left arm?"

Claudette glared up at Horace now, studying his face as he winced and gulped against a stifled scream.

"I didn't want her to die," Horace squeaked. "I just wanted her to break a leg or something, so she'd stop showing me up when she climbed that tree. I was a kid. I didn't know she'd die."

"What about your baby?" Raleigh asked. "It's her cry you can hear sometimes when the house is quiet."

Horace trembled. He appeared in danger of not being able to stand much longer. "I froze. I wanted to help, but all I could see was Claudette's face."

Claudette glanced over at Raleigh, her head tilted. The grip of anger on her young, delicate features had slackened.

"Well, Sissy," Mathis said. "It seems your spawn have spiraled out of control. You may be in danger here."

"But you sir," Raleigh said, turning on him, "are the one trying to steal the house by putting Eliza in a retirement home."

"Concern for my sister, I assure you," Mathis said.

"Or for yourself?" Raleigh asked. "Remember there are two ghost girls who can tell me what you did to them."

"Absurd," Mathis said. "No one will believe the word of two ghosts or someone who claims to speak to them, so watch how you malign my impeccable character."

"Except isn't that why your father sent you away?" Raleigh said. "Isn't that why he disinherited you during a time when you were guaranteed to inherit this place as well as the trust that maintains the home?"

"You are just trying to rattle me," Mathis said. "I'm not as foolish as my nephew."

Eliza took two steps closer to her brother. "What did you do to my girls?"

"Sissy, calm down," Mathis said, putting a hand up. "This

young lady is reaching. No need to get you worked up. It's not good for your health."

Eliza waved him away. "I'm not an invalid, and you are ten years older than me. Nor am I as oblivious as you two believe I am. I know you were keeping something from me. What is it exactly?"

"You've heard it already," Mathis said, sternly. "Your son tried to steal your home."

Horace clenched his fist. "You molested those girls. You probably did it to my mother and that's why you lost what you believe is yours."

With a downcast face, Eliza tapped her cane down on the floor hard. "I've heard enough for today. We are celebrating a wedding, not delving into our dark family secrets. Joey, can you take these two far from our property? I'd prefer not to ruin my grandson's wedding."

Joey shifted forward. "Squad car's waiting out front. We have a few questions for you two down at the station."

"For a canceled caterer?" Horace squawked.

"For the attempt on the lives of the priest, bride and groom, and for conning an elderly woman from her property."

Horace glared at his uncle. Mathis's anger had darkened his face, and if his health would allow, he certainly would have pushed his way past them.

Joey motioned toward the door. "Let's go gentlemen."

The men left without any further comment, although Horace looked longingly toward his mother as if for forgiveness. Eliza did not look their way, only to the spot where Raleigh had indicated Claudette stood.

Except now Claudette stood by her mother's side as if sensing her pain and feeling a need to protect her.

"I suspected the girls still resided here," Eliza said, her voice low and throaty. "About twenty years ago, we had this physic visit from New Orleans. My husband was alive then, of course, and he believed it to all be a hoax, but she did this reading for the dinner party. She told me, well the entire table really, that the spirits of children ran amuck around the house. My husband thought it ludicrous, but..."

"You believed it was the girls," Raleigh said.

Eliza nodded. "I put twin beds in Claudette's old room. My husband thought it was for our grandkids, but then I wouldn't let them sleep in it. And then later, your Me 'Maw came to visit one of our housekeepers to bring her some vegetables, and she asked about a crying baby. And I realized that all three of the girls must be here, so I added the bassinet from the attic. My husband believed I had gone insane and refused to go upstairs anymore."

"But you've never seen them?" Raleigh asked.

"No," Eliza responded, sighing. "But I think it may be enough now that I know for sure that they are here, that you can see them."

Raleigh smiled. "I don't think Claudette has any plans on leaving."

Eliza moved toward a wing back chair and leaned on it for support. "I suppose it's selfish of me to be good with that choice for now, but maybe one day we can talk about helping her move onto whatever is beyond this existence. A better place."

"My Aunt Clarice shares a house with me, and it's unlikely she ever moves on willingly. Sometimes they have their own thoughts on the subject," Raleigh said.

Eliza's shoulders slumped. "This is a big house to live in all alone. Perhaps I will need them just to fill the emptiness."

"I'm sure you will figure out something useful to do with all of this space," Raleigh said. "But I do have to ask you to keep the baby news quiet at least until New Year's Day. There's this big reveal plan in place."

Eliza looked around the room, still unaware of her daughter standing near her. "A girl, huh? A bit of good news on an otherwise day of dreadful turns. Perhaps the Manor won't be empty for long."

"Let's get back to the wedding before Sheri begins to look for me," Raleigh said. She figured Sheri and Jeff's desire for anything to do with this house after the last three days of Christmas "miracles" could be left to tomorrow's problem. Not by her, of course. The family could take over after the last bite of cake had been served this evening.

CHAPTER FOURTEEN

Raleigh sat on the floor, nursing her lukewarm coffee, and staring at the Christmas tree that she had spent little time with this year. Last year, with her first year in this house, they'd had a hub of activity all season long. In fact, at this time last year, the entire crew had been over sharing Papa Noel stockings and a breakfast casserole. She'd figured they would have a few more years before the group dynamics shifted.

But this year, Madison had to supervise some of the clean up after last night's New Year's Eve parties, so Mason and her sister's stockings sat untouched until they could make it over. Mason would be asleep at her parents, having asked to stay up until midnight last night. He'd almost made it. Jeff, Sheri, and Shawn's stockings also hung untouched as they'd be returning from their honeymoon today, but they had a family obligation and may not make it to Raleigh's house. Winter's stocking would hang unclaimed until next week when she returned from rehab. And Raleigh hadn't had the heart to open stockings with just her and Mike.

Luna shifted her head on her lap and perked up her ears.

She sprung to her feet, and her nails were taping against the wooden floor moments before the doorbell rang.

Mike shuffled from the back kitchen where he'd been putting his final touches on a dump cake. Raleigh had been quite leery when he first mentioned this sweet, but it was some recipe his mother typically made for New Year's Day, and he wanted to contribute to the family gathering at Me'Maw's just like everyone else.

Mason sprinted inside with Luna barking at his feet. Her nephew ran straight to his stocking, snatching it from the holder on the old gas radiator where Raleigh had hung his.

"Well, hello to you too, favorite nephew," Raleigh said.

Mason giggled. "I'm too excited, Nanan. I can't wait to see what Papa Noel brought me. I have plenty time for your hugs."

Mason flipped the Christmas stocking upside down, spilling its contents onto the rug.

He yelped with joy as he scooped up the specialty, colored pencils. He'd recently been sketching rudimentary drawings of trees and plants. The scribbles and scratches showed some promise, at least Raleigh could decipher his intended subject. She'd stuffed those inside the stocking to encourage him to continue.

"Papa Noel knows everything!" Mason exclaimed.

Madison breezed in, lowering her dark shades. "Yes, remember that he also sees when you are sneaking cookies into bed when you should be asleep."

Mason giggled as he sorted through the candy and trinkets she and Madison had stuffed inside. Mason had received another stocking at their parents' home, but Madison claimed this one as her contribution. Their mother put so many items inside his one at their house that it didn't leave space for Madison to contribute. The entire friendship stocking tradition had sprung up last year because she and her sister had decided that Raleigh's house would offer them control for Mason as well as their adult friends who didn't have families of their own yet. Everyone would stuff a little something for each other. This last Christmas festivity of the season would begin the new year off on a positive note for everyone.

Now that they'd made it through the wedding, Raleigh's wish for the new year was for less obstacles with more enjoyment with her friends. Perhaps she'd even sample Me'Maw's field peas and cabbage today. She could never remember which one was supposed to bring luck and which one money. She could probably use a little of both these days.

The doorbell rang again. Mike hadn't walked completely into the living room before he turned to answer the door. He even whistled as he walked there. In all the years she'd known him, this was the least stressed he'd been for the holiday. He'd politely refused his mother's invitation to lunch, insisting that they'd drop in for a visit later in the afternoon. He'd even extended his family an invitation to celebrate at Me'Maw's and Paw's, which they'd also politely refused. Paw had always teased Mike about wanting to be a Cheramie, and Raleigh could say that he seemed happier having embraced the idea.

Mike returned followed by Sheri and Jeff.

Shawn ran past all three, sprinting toward his own stocking hanging on the radiator.

Raleigh laughed, warmth washing over her. The small family of friends she'd built had all made it together after all. Perhaps this year wouldn't be as different as she thought.

Standing to hug her friend, she asked Sheri, "How was the honeymoon?"

Sheri smiled, her face beaming.

Raleigh laughed. "Share the blue water and drinks by the pool only."

Jeff braced himself as Mason ran and jumped on him.

Lifting the boy up like Superman, Jeff tossed Mason in the air. Mason giggled in delight.

"Our cabana boy Reeco had excellent service. I am now sad to go back and live like a peasant, not to mention having to attend the big family lunch at Eliza's house today," Sheri said.

"Do they know about the baby yet?" Madison asked, watching Mason come down from his precarious position.

Sheri nodded. "Our Papa Noel announcements worked wonderful except for all the calls we have been receiving since we landed at the airport this morning."

Jeff stood, stretching his back now. "We wanted to see if you had changed your minds about joining us at the Dantin Manor for lunch."

Mike chuckled. "And miss Me'Maw's cooking?"

Jeff laughed. "I knew it was a long shot, but I had to ask. Both of our families will be there, and I'm guessing we are in for just as much trouble as the Christmas dinner."

Mason had returned to his stocking, so Madison dropped to the edge of Aunt Clarice's chair. Raleigh had noticed a new level of hovering since the wedding and Mason's talent reveal. "Not possible. They will be in the baby bubble for at least a few days if not weeks. Everyone will be excited and extra nice."

A worry line creased Sheri's forehead. "I hope so."

Raleigh said, "No more worrying about some nonexistent family curse. You need to enjoy this time."

"Well," Sheri said, looking toward Jeff. "We have a favor to ask you and Mike."

"What's that?" Mike asked.

"Would you be the baby's godparents?" Jeff asked with a grin.

Nausea and joy struck Raleigh all at once. This baby had been plenty of work already, and the diva hadn't made her entrance yet. She sure hoped godmother duties didn't include saving her life every week.

Mike bear hugged Raleigh from behind and squeezed. "Of course, we will."

Raleigh nodded, knowing she'd take on the responsibility no matter what.

Madison laughed. "Raleigh's the fairy godmother of saving babies these days. Who knows, might be her own next."

Raleigh grimaced at her, a look she'd offered her sister often growing up. Southerners reserved the expression "Bless your heart" for people like Madison, but Raleigh would prefer to use the not so polite words when dealing with her sister.

Jeff cleared his throat. "Do you think maybe you could get the girls of the manor to move on?"

"Claudette's not going anywhere. At least not as long as her mother is there," Raleigh said. "Rebecca may leave eventually. But they really are harmless and weren't responsible for any of it."

Jeff nodded. "I know. My father's helping Eliza get everything straight now. It's just strange knowing they are there."

"You know what?" Mike said, releasing Raleigh. "Let's follow through with our traditions before we all scatter. I'll get what we need for a toast."

Sheri pointed to her belly, which had rounded out some just in the last week. "No alcohol right now, remember?"

Mike shook his head before disappearing down the hall. A minute later he returned with a stack of plastic cups and a bottle of sparkling cider he'd bought yesterday to create some type of punch for their New Year's Eve celebration. They'd ended up curled up on the sofa with Luna and too comfortable to move. They'd both been exhausted after the wedding and having to return to work.

Jeff helped him pass out the cups, Mike popped the cork, and everyone raised their glasses.

"To friends who are our family," Mike said, looking around the group.

Sheri added. "To growing healthy families with the help of our friends."

"To the mushiness," Madison said, pulling her cup away. "I sure do miss Winter."

Raleigh smiled. It was nice to see the softer side of her sister, even when it came with her biting sarcasm.

"I'll get your stockings!" Mason yelled. "I can't wait to see what Papa Noel brought you!"

Shawn dropped his own stocking and rushed to help him.

Everyone laughed.

Raleigh didn't know what the new year would bring, but she imagined the dead weren't going away. As long as she could enjoy the living, she'd make her peace with it.

ACKNOWLEDGMENTS

Though this story takes place in a fictional world, it is a conglomerate of the places of my childhood memories. I consult the people around me continuously to keep the perspective of South Louisiana. I also want to thank those who offered stories and help along the way in keeping the Cajun aspects authentic.

AUTHOR

JESSICA TASTET is the author of eight novels and a children's story. She's worked in education for twenty-four years and as an editor for six years. She lives in Louisiana with her family.

For updates visit:
   www.jessicatastet.com

www.ingramcontent.com/pod-product-compliance
Lightning Source LLC
Chambersburg PA
CBHW071135200626
46817CB00018B/3016